Dark Delusion

A Maryanne Mystery

Rosemary Gemmell

To Jeannie,
Hope you enjoy!
Best wishes,
Rosemary Gemmell
X

Dark Delusion

A responsive influence exists between the heavenly bodies, the earth, and animated bodies.
Franz Anton Mesmer

Chapter One

Maryanne opened her curtains with a sense of anticipation mingled with apprehension. The morning rays of the sun cast light across the hills visible from the parsonage window. A good day for travelling before the long winter arrived again.

It would be her first visit to Mulberry Manor since the events of that memorable Twelfth Night of 1859; well over a year ago. How would her cousin Charlotte fair by now? The most recent communication Maryanne had received from Emily suggested some concern about her sister but with no further details in the letter. She must curb her impatience until she arrived and trust that it was nothing too dreadful.

Her own fortunes were undergoing change, now that Richard had made it clear he wished to marry her. Her heart warmed at the memory of his kisses at Carmichael Hall last Christmas. Even the dreadful events of that visit could not dim her happiness.

Her sojourn at Mulberry Manor would be short this time, before she and Emily travelled to London. She could scarcely wait to venture into the capital city, not least since they would be meeting their beloveds there. No doubt Richard may already have organised a few outings for them and Maryanne imagined that Emily must share her excitement.

Her aunt had arranged for them to stay at the town house of her widowed cousin, Lady Malden, who was famous for her soirées and evidently mixed with the most interesting intellectuals in London. Maryanne looked forward to meeting her and hoped she might make the acquaintance of at least one scientist.

Meanwhile, she carefully packed her journal and writings on astronomy gleaned from the newspaper, especially anything pertaining to Mary Somerville. It was satisfying to note how well she was now received amongst the echelons of London astronomical society. Maryanne might never attain such expertise or learning herself but appreciated the fact that a Scottish *woman* had infiltrated such lofty establishments.

Once packed, she allowed her thoughts to dwell on Richard once more. Although they were officially affianced, no date had yet been set for their marriage and she hoped nothing untoward might come between them this time. No doubt she would soon receive all the news regarding her cousin Henry and his friendship with Miss King and her recovered child.

A knock on her bedroom door reminded her the carriage was due at any moment and she must take her leave of Mama and Papa, both of whom were happily content in their small parish in the Scottish Borders.

"Are you ready, Maryanne?" Her mother's gentle voice called.

"Come in, Mama. I think I've remembered everything I shall need."

"Very well. We shall miss you, daughter. Be careful of those robbers and worse in London. Make certain you are never alone in the streets."

"I promise to be vigilant, Mama. Please don't worry about me."

Maryanne embraced her mother, taking the older

woman by surprise. Her parents were not nearly as demonstrative as her aunt and uncle at Mulberry Manor, but they loved each other dearly. They worked hard to ensure the parishioners were well looked after, in body by her mother and in spirit by her reverend father.

Soon, she was on her way, her maid, Timmy, in the carriage beside her, excited at being reunited with the cousins' maid at Mulberry Manor for a short time. She would not be accompanying Maryanne and Emily to London by train, however. Lady Malden had offered one of her own maids for their use in London and Timmy would return to the parsonage to be of help where needed.

"Is London very big, Miss?" Timmy asked, as the carriage swayed on the rougher roads.

"Very. And I believe it's noisy and dirty and quite unlike any place we have seen before."

"Is this your first visit then, Miss?"

"I'm afraid it is, and one I have longed for ever since the Great Exhibition some years ago. I do wish I'd been able to attend its opening but, alas, I was too young and too poor to travel so far."

She smiled to take away any complaint in her words. Both her statements were true but at least she might be able to visit the Crystal Palace, if at all possible.

"I'd love to see it all one day, Miss."

"And so you shall, Timmy."

Maryanne said no more, but perhaps when she married, Timmy could become her proper personal maid and leave her other small tasks at the parsonage behind. Her dear Mama and Papa had been determined their daughter would have some kind of maid and would manage very well with their other help.

Both lapsed into silence as they passed through the pleasant green countryside. Maryanne caught sight of the wisps of smoke from a steam train in the distance. That was another pleasure she was very soon to experience, now that the railways had expanded even more.

Maryanne admired the autumn russet, gold and ochre shades as they neared Mulberry Manor, glad this short visit was not in winter like last time, although she loved the cold frosty days if not travelling about the countryside. And she always received a warm welcome at the manor.

As soon as she reached the large oak door, it opened to reveal her aunt and uncle, who never waited on ceremony, hovering behind the footman.

"Maryanne, my darling niece, welcome, welcome. Come in."

Once ushered inside, Maryanne made sure that Timmy was given directions before properly greeting her aunt and uncle.

"My, you're even prettier than I remember. Doubtless a certain handsome young man has something to do with that." Her aunt held out her arms once she'd paused talking long enough.

Enveloped in a tight embrace from both aunt and uncle, Maryanne smiled, glad to be released but full of happiness at such exuberance. They could not be more different from her own parents and she marvelled again that her mother and aunt were sisters.

"I'm delighted to be here, Aunt, Uncle, and thank

you for such a warm welcome. Mama and Papa send their best regards."

"Well now, I expect you'll want to get settled. Emily can scarcely contain her impatience to see you. I've put you in the same room as previously, if that suits you well enough?"

Maryanne didn't miss the note of anxiety in her aunt's question, but she was perfectly certain that no ghosts now walked the corridors of Mulberry Manor.

"Of course it is, thank you."

Before she could take another step, Emily came rushing towards her.

"Maryanne! Oh, it's so good to see you again. Isn't it exciting to be visiting London? I'm so impatient to be on our way."

Returning Emily's tight hug, Maryanne reflected that in several years from now, Emily would no doubt resemble her kind-hearted mother even more, though not perhaps in girth.

"It's a pleasure to be here, dear cousin. How are your sister and brother?"

"Henry is very well and we may even see him in London as he's down there just now. Charlotte is looking forward to seeing you but is in her room at present."

Maryanne caught the glance that passed between the three people standing around her and knew something was still amiss with the elder daughter of the house.

"Come upstairs and see your room, Maryanne. It has new curtains since your last visit and is much brighter."

Understanding that Emily wished to speak to her

on her own as quickly as possible, Maryanne followed her upstairs after a quick thank you to her aunt and uncle.

When she entered the generous sized bedroom, Maryanne had a fleeting memory of the night she had seen what could only be described as a spirit or ghost. But that was in the past and unlikely to bother any of them again. Except perhaps the lingering problems with Charlotte? She had suffered the most and seemed unable to forget the experience, as far as she surmised.

"The room is lovely and bright indeed, Emily, although I suspect it always looks better before the dark days of winter. Now come and tell me how you are and if you've heard recently from George."

A pretty blush coloured Emily's cheeks as she sat beside Maryanne on the bed.

"I have and he is very well. He and Richard seem to be settled in their temporary home in London for now and are looking forward to our visit. George hinted that they have several outings planned and I do hope one of them is to the theatre or music hall!"

Excitement came easily to her cousin but Maryanne could not deny her own joyful expectation of being taken out by the brothers who had captured their hearts. She too hoped for entertainment of some kind. Although her own preference would be for a talk on science or astronomy perhaps, the theatre would also be quite acceptable.

For now, however, her curiosity was for Charlotte and she could not wait any longer to find out what was bothering the family.

"And your sister? Is Charlotte well?"

Emily took a moment before answering then she

shrugged. "I don't think so, Maryanne, but I'm not quite sure what ails her. She is being most secretive, even more than usual, and I've noticed a correspondence arrive for her now and then. She always makes certain to look at the mail before Papa can reach it but will not share the contents. Who could possibly be writing to my sister?"

Maryanne had to admit she was equally bemused but could offer no solution. "She has given you no clue at all? Presumably she writes in return?"

"She scarcely acknowledges my questions and, yes, I do believe she posts a letter in return but is careful not to let me glimpse the name or address. How can she be so secretive with me?"

Maryanne took Emily's hand. "Perhaps she knows it might distress you or that you would immediately tell your parents. Do you think she might confide in me, if I do not ask too many questions?"

Emily's face brightened. "Oh, please do try, Maryanne. She no doubt finds me irritating at times as she is so much quieter than me, and I admit I do talk rather a lot about George and our future together."

Maryanne had to laugh at Emily's self-awareness and had no doubt her chatter might make Charlotte speak even less. She could try to gain her cousin's confidence, although she had never been as close to her as to Emily. Yet Charlotte had welcomed Maryanne's quiet good sense after the ghostly incident. Perhaps she would value a confidante who did not live in the same house.

"Then it is settled. We leave for London in two days, so allow me to try and have a walk with Charlotte around the grounds before then and I'll do my best to find out what I can."

Chapter Two

At first sight, Charlotte appeared well, if a little thinner, welcoming Maryanne as warmly as the rest of the family.

"How lovely to see you again, cousin. Emily told me all about your exciting adventure at Christmas, though I must confess I'm happy I remained here."

"It was certainly not what we expected from our visit to Carmichael Hall but your brother was one of the heroes."

Charlotte laughed as she took Maryanne's arm while they continued their stroll around the gardens of Mulberry Manor.

"Good for Henry! I believe he still keeps in touch with Miss King, although he does not share his plans with his sisters."

Maryanne admired the shrubs and trees that had graced these grounds for centuries, remembering long-ago visits when she had longed to climb into the branches of the tallest tree and survey the countryside. But today, she must try and find out more about Charlotte's secret correspondence, as she had promised Emily, although she must tread carefully.

However, it was Charlotte herself who allowed a way in to the conversation. She stopped on the path beside a rowan tree still ripe with red berries not already eaten by the birds.

"Maryanne, I would like to accompany you and

Emily to London, if you will not mind."

Surprised by the suggestion, Maryanne took a moment to reply.

"Well, I expect that will be possible if your mama has no objection. Do you mean to stay with us at Lady Malden's town house?"

Charlotte hesitated, a frown creasing her normally smooth brow. "Why, yes, of course, if she will not mind another guest."

"Does Emily know of your plans?"

Charlotte shook her head. "Not yet. I hoped you might mention it to her first. She has a tendency to ask too many questions to which I have no answers."

Maryanne frowned at such an unsatisfactory reply, aware that the girl was not about to confide in her either. What could Charlotte possibly have to hide? Yet her family would no doubt be relieved that she was venturing away from the manor at all.

"I think that is enough walking for today," Charlotte said.

Maryanne tried to think of a way to find out more before they returned to the house as she might not have another chance.

"Is there anything in particular you would like to see while in London, Charlotte? I'm hoping that Richard and George might escort us to one or two amusements."

Charlotte continued strolling without speaking for a moment. She turned to Maryanne, taking her by surprise when she clutched at her hands.

"You must not say anything, Maryanne. Promise me, or I will remain silent."

Reluctant to give such a promise but, aware she

was being offered at least some confidence, Maryanne agreed.

"I promise for now, Charlotte." That was as far as she could go until she knew more.

After a longer hesitation, while Maryanne remained as patient as possible, Charlotte nodded.

"There is one type of meeting that I hope to visit, but Mama and Papa must not know. I wish to see a demonstration of mesmerism."

Whatever Maryanne had expected, this was the very last thing she imagined her cousin would want anything to do with, after her previous experience.

"But why on earth would you wish to attend such a meeting?" Another thought came to her. "And how do you know it might be possible?"

Charlotte started walking again and would not look at Maryanne.

"I am corresponding with someone in London who is interested in such practises."

Maryanne was about to ask if she might know the name of this person, but Charlotte turned anguished eyes on her and clutched at her hands again.

"Please, Maryanne, do not try to dissuade me for I must know more about this. I've not been myself since those terrible events at the manor when you visited for Twelfth Night, and the only way in which I might begin to progress is to understand my fears."

Maryanne embraced her distressed cousin before replying. How sad that Charlotte had kept these feelings to herself for so long.

"First of all, dear cousin, I'm sorry you've been so affected all this time and I do think a visit to the city might be the very thing for you. However, I cannot keep secrets from Emily if we're to be together in London. You must promise not to go anywhere by yourself as we don't know the dangers that might lurk for a young lady on her own."

Charlotte brushed a tear from her eyes. "I will not go anywhere unescorted and, indeed, you and Emily are welcome to attend any such meeting with me."

Maryanne made no reply until she could ponder more about the situation, and had to be content with Charlotte's agreement. She was aware of its ambiguity, however, and had the strongest suspicion that the girl had quite another escort in mind.

As they approached the house, Maryanne allowed Charlotte to change the subject and compose herself before facing her family. But she squeezed the girl's hand reassuringly and was rewarded with a smile. It would have to suffice for now, but the visit to London might prove more of a challenge than she had expected.

Chapter Three

Charlotte's parents were so overjoyed their elder daughter was finally venturing away from Mulberry Manor again that Maryanne hid her concern regarding the reason for Charlotte's sudden wish to travel as far as London.

When Maryanne had told her younger cousin about Charlotte's request to accompany them, Emily had been astonished that her sister had never confided in her and worried that the journey might prove too much after so long remaining at home.

"We shall have to ensure that Charlotte is under our gentle supervision while in the city," Maryanne suggested. "Without causing her anxiety, of course."

"Well, I must admit I'm happy to see my dear sister taking an interest in anything at last. But, yes, we must be careful of her, for although Charlotte can be most stubborn, she is also still vulnerable, I think. It's so long since she's been in company that I cannot imagine why she should choose London of all places."

Maryanne merely agreed. She had decided not to mention Charlotte's proposed visit to a mesmerism demonstration until she discovered more about it. She was still convinced that her cousin fully intended to meet the person with whom she had been corresponding.

As they set out in the carriage to the railway station, Maryanne allowed herself to dwell on the excitement of her first train journey, as well as the pleasant anticipation of seeing Richard again. She hoped there would be no unexpected young lady on his arm this time. Emily, too, was looking out of the window, no doubt thinking of George.

Charlotte had been quiet since they left Mulberry Manor and Maryanne hoped she was not regretting her decision already. Yet there was a nervous excitement about the girl and Maryanne tried to draw her into conversation, hoping to glean something about her thoughts.

"We're very pleased to have your company, Charlotte. No doubt your brother will be delighted to see you again and you may even meet Miss King. Richard and George promised some entertainment for us and I'm hoping a visit to the theatre is included."

"Oh, that would be delightful," Emily agreed. "Do you not think so, Charlotte?"

It took Charlotte a moment to turn her attention to them, as though her mind had been far away.

"That would be very pleasant, I expect. There are so many gatherings one might visit in London and I do hope to visit one or two." She met Maryanne's gaze and gave a secretive little smile.

Maryanne's heart was full of misgivings at having not told Emily everything about her conversation with Charlotte. She would remedy that at the earliest opportunity to ensure her cousin was under supervision at all times.

All three girls stepped onto the huge train with some excitement. Thankfully, a porter took care of their luggage and ensured they were safely settled into a furnished first-class carriage, secured for them in advance by Maryanne's aunt and uncle.

"Did you see the dirty smoke?" Emily asked, eyes wide at all the sights. "But isn't it exciting and so romantic seeing the huge engine appear through the steam!"

"I'm afraid the soot is one disadvantage of steam, but I do agree it's very exciting." Maryanne smiled at Emily.

She was amazed at the crowds of people already travelling this way, and the journey afforded them an interesting view of the passing countryside and towns.

But their northern departure station had been small compared to the vast King's Cross Station in London when they arrived.

As well as the noisy hustle and bustle of travellers coming and going, suitcases and trunks stood ready to be loaded and Maryanne even caught sight of mail bags being thrown onto one railway carriage.

She wished Charlotte had shown even a little more enthusiasm on the journey, but she had remained mostly silent since the carriage, her thoughts obviously elsewhere.

London was as noisy and dirty as Maryanne expected when they finally reached the heart of the city. The dome of St Paul's cathedral rose up from narrow streets and large buildings, while carriages, horses, carts, beggar children and street sellers added to the cacophony of sound. Maryanne had never been to such an exciting place before and she couldn't stop smiling at the sights as a carriage transported them from the station to their destination.

Emily was equally eager to see as much as possible

from the inadequate carriage windows.

"Oh, look at that street sweeper," she cried out. "He's only a child and that horse and carriage almost ran into him!"

"I expect he'll be used to these streets and is able to look out for such hazards," Charlotte said, without any of her sister's sympathy.

Maryanne smiled to herself. Already, Charlotte sounded more like the person she had spent time with at Mulberry Manor, before the ghostly events that had left the poor girl in fear of her life. Perhaps this time away from the house was exactly what Charlotte needed.

Lady Malden's house in Grosvenor Square was as grand as those of her neighbours, as befitted her position in society and as the wealthy widow of a member of the aristocracy. A footman answered their arrival and welcomed them into the parlour, assuring them that Lady Malden was expecting them. He bowed and closed the door behind them, allowing Maryanne the opportunity to approve the lady's taste in this room at least.

The door opened again with a flourish as Lady Malden entered the room, arms outstretched, a smile on her handsome face.

"My dears, how delightful to welcome you to my home. I do love young company and I expect you will be excited to see what London has to offer."

Maryanne, Emily and Charlotte were about to curtsy but were each grasped firmly and kissed on both cheeks.

"You must be Maryanne," Lady Malden said, standing back to appraise her. "I have heard much about you and cannot wonder that young Richard Carmichael is already smitten."

Before Maryanne could calm the blush that crept over her cheeks, or think how to reply, Lady Malden had already moved on to Charlotte.

"I am very pleased you decided to join the other young ladies, my dear. It's too long since I've seen you and Emily." She took a hand of both the sisters. "You are grown so beautiful, although your cheeks are a little pinched, Charlotte. Never mind, you shall enjoy your visit here."

Maryanne hid a smile at such confidence, suspecting that Lady Malden was a force of nature who would carry them all along in whatever plans she concocted for their amusement. Still a commandingly handsome woman in mid-life, widowhood obviously had not diminished the lady's personality and her tall stature was both imposing yet not too slender to hide her femininity.

"Thank you for such a warm welcome, Lady Malden. Mama and Papa send their regards and grateful thanks for accommodating us," Emily said.

"May I too say thank you, Lady Malden, as I have never been to London before," Maryanne added.

"Now that's enough of the Lady Malden. You must all call me Aunt Drusilla while here. I shall introduce you as my nieces to save confusion or unnecessary explanations as to our relationship."

Turning to ring one of the bells on the wall, the lady continued. "I expect you wish to see your rooms and freshen up after your journey. My own maid and her young assistant shall attend to your needs. We shall dine at home this evening, but with several invited guests. I trust that will suit you well enough for today."

Content to be shown a room to herself by the friendly housekeeper who had answered the bell summons, Maryanne surveyed her surroundings. Although not as large a space as the room at Mulberry Manor, this one was much brighter and prettier with a pleasant view of the wide street below. The high bed looked comfortable and she noticed a chamber pot beneath, while along one wall stood a blue stand with a marble top which held a pretty basin and jug for her ablutions. A clothes press stood in one corner ready to receive those few gowns she had brought with her, a set of drawers beside it for other garments.

A knock on her door proved to be a young maid who offered to unpack Maryanne's clothes. "I'm Simmons, Miss, and will be looking after you."

"Thank you, Simmons. I will be very glad of your assistance when required. We are to dine in this evening with invited guests, so perhaps the pink gown might be appropriate?"

Simmons was already hanging up the gowns and she nodded. "Lovely, Miss, an' I can do your hair in a pretty style."

Once her belongings were unpacked, and Simmons had filled the jug with warm water for Maryanne to wash, she was left by herself to mull over the coming evening. Her heart quickened at thought of seeing Richard again and she longed for the day when they might always be together at last.

Maryanne was no sooner dressed in her finery, her hair in a simple chignon, when Emily knocked on her door, still excited at being in London. Before going downstairs, Maryanne looked for Charlotte but her door was still firmly closed.

"I'd better knock to see if your sister is ready," Maryanne said.

"Oh, don't bother, Maryanne. I already checked and Charlotte told us to go on." She lowered her voice. "I hope she isn't regretting the journey already."

They had turned towards the staircase when they heard Charlotte's door open.

"I suppose I'd better come with you so I don't upset Lady Malden on the first day here," she said.

Maryanne and Emily stared at the picture Charlotte made in a hooped fine muslin evening gown embroidered with tiny flowers around the hem and neck.

"Why, I've not seen you look so pretty for too long, sister," Emily cried.

"I must agree how beautiful you look, Charlotte." Maryanne was both relieved that her cousin had dressed so well and amazed at the change from the slightly surly girl who had accompanied them in the carriage.

Charlotte gave a small smile. "Thank you. I might as well make the most of my time here."

Rather than wait for the others to lead the way, Charlotte swept ahead, back straight, head high.

Maryanne and Emily looked at each other, eyebrows raised, before following. Maryanne suspected she would see many sides to Charlotte before the visit was over.

"Ah, there you are, my dears. You know our first two gentlemen guests already, of course." Lady Malden welcomed the three girls into the drawing room.

Maryanne's gaze went immediately to Richard Carmichael and she had to contain her longing to run straight to his side. Emily was equally delighted to see George and had no such qualms, making her way directly to him.

"Maryanne, how good to finally see you again."

Richard bowed to her at once before turning his surprised gaze on Charlotte. "Miss Harrington, I had not expected to see you here. How do you do?"

Charlotte curtsied and turned her full attention on Richard. "Fie, Richard, you know me well enough to use my given name, especially if you are to be my brother-in-law."

Emily gasped at such indiscretion, her face reddening as she looked at her sister then at George. "Charlotte! How can you embarrass us so?"

George laughed. "You sister speaks the truth, Emily. And I hope that day will not be too far off."

Maryanne met Richard's gaze and was glad when he changed the subject away from any talk of their possible matrimony. That was for their ears only when the opportunity arose.

"You are well, Charlotte?" Richard asked.

"Perfectly well, thank you."

Charlotte turned away as though to dismiss all boring talk of her health, allowing Maryanne a few moments with Richard. But George had an announcement.

"We must tell you, ladies, that we're to visit the theatre in two nights time," George said, his smile still for Emily.

She did not disappoint, clapping her hands in delight. "How wonderful. You must tell us more before the evening ends."

At that moment, the footman announced another guest and everyone turned with interest to see who had come amongst them.

The woman was neither in the first flush of youth nor elderly, but certainly beautiful. Her burnished hair was elegantly swept above a high forehead, her neat figure encased in a deep midnight blue gown that spoke of wealth, even without the sparkling diamond necklace around her pale neck, cleverly placed to draw attention to a magnificent bosom above the low neckline of the gown.

Maryanne was not surprised that all eyes watched as the lady approached with the utmost confidence to greet her hostess.

"Lady Malden, it is a pleasure to be here again."

"Welcome, Lady Grey, it's always a pleasure to welcome you here. Now let us dispense with formality, Carolyn. Come and meet my nieces."

Their chatter was soon interrupted when two other guests were announced to claim their interest.

"Ah, Madame Juliette. Welcome. Please come and meet my other guests." Lady Malden seemed genuinely pleased to see the woman who at once commanded attention.

Maryanne smiled into intelligent dark eyes as she greeted the new arrival and received an effusive greeting in return. She was certainly an arresting sight, with hair as black as coal, lustrous dark lashes and a lavish low-cut crimson gown that ensured she would never be overlooked. Rubies clung to her neck and ears as though made for her and Maryanne noticed that every man in the room seemed enchanted by her.

"Thank you, dear Lady Malden. It is my great pleasure to attend your soirée, and to meet such a delightful group of people."

She paused as though remembering the man who stood just inside the drawing room door, a look of amusement that was almost a sneer marring his otherwise pleasant face.

"May I present Mr William Taylor."

Lady Malden inclined her head. "How do you do, Mr Taylor? You are very welcome here."

Maryanne watched as the young man bowed over Lady Malden's hand, noticing the way in which his gaze lingered a little too long as he straightened, that half smile still evident.

"You are most kind, thank you. And I see you have a pretty collection of young ladies brightening the room this evening."

Maryanne bristled at his tone and was not surprised when Richard moved closer to her. Mr Taylor's whole demeanour suggested the kind of predatory male that young ladies were warned against. She had to admit, however, that he was a handsome enough young man and perhaps she was too hasty in her judgment as to his character.

On being introduced to them, he was polite towards Maryanne and Emily, which perhaps had something to do with Richard and George making their allegiance clear. Charlotte, however, was another matter entirely and Maryanne noticed at once the flirtatious flick of her cousin's fan as she curtsied.

"Delighted to make your acquaintance, Miss Harrington," Mr Taylor said, smiling into Charlotte's eyes a little longer than necessary.

His pleasant voice was cultured but something in his manner warned Maryanne he might be less respectful of young ladies than she would like.

"And I yours, Mr Taylor," Charlotte replied, boldly meeting his gaze.

Madame Juliette had also noticed the little exchange, Maryanne surmised, as she watched with interest.

"William and I mean to take every opportunity to visit the theatre and such like while in London. Perhaps we might make a party of it one evening," Madame Juliette suggested.

She had placed her hand on Mr Taylor's arm as though to claim him for herself. Maryanne wondered what their relationship could be since the lady was many years older than the young man.

"Splendid!" the ever-pleasant George replied. "Matter of fact, we'll be visiting the Adelphi theatre in two night's time."

"Now that sounds a delightful idea," Mr Taylor said, his gaze straying to Charlotte again.

Maryanne turned her attention to Madame Juliette who continued watching with an indulgent smile. She had expected the exotic-looking lady to have a foreign accent, but she spoke in perfectly modulated English. Perhaps she was an actress and her name was assumed for that reason?

Her unspoken question was answered almost at once.

"Madame Juliette has a special gift that we hope she will share with us later in the evening. She is one of our more acclaimed spiritualists," Lady Malden said.

"And greatly sought after in certain circles," Lady Grey affirmed.

Maryanne wondered if she were the only person to hear the small gasp from Charlotte, but Richard caught her eye and she knew he had observed Charlotte's reaction. But was it distress or excitement that made the girl's eyes widen? Maryanne had the distinct impression that her cousin's interest was piqued.

"You are too kind, Lady Malden, but I would certainly enjoy a little experiment if no one objects." Madame Juliette turned her charm on all those gathered and smiled when there was no voice of dissent.

Conversation resumed in small groups while they mingled.

"I wonder if this is a good idea," Richard said at Maryanne's side.

Maryanne turned her back to the room so she might converse with him more quietly for a moment.

"Exactly what I was thinking, but we are only guests in this house and there is little we can do without embarrassing Charlotte. And I'm not quite certain she is against whatever experiment the lady has in mind."

"Then we shall await events and be prepared to intervene if necessary. Now enough about your cousin. How are you, my dearest heart?"

Maryanne put her hand in his and Richard pressed a kiss on her palm that sent a shiver of delight through her.

"I am very well, thank you, and even better for seeing you again." She reclaimed her hand before anyone noticed, fanning her warm face.

"We must steal a little time alone, Maryanne, for

we have serious matters to discuss." His smile told her they were the kind of serious matters she too wanted to discuss.

At that moment, dinner was announced, bringing their intimate conversation to an end while they took their places in the large dining room.

Pleased to be seated beside Richard on one side, Maryanne was surprised to find Mr Taylor on her other. However, it was soon evident that Charlotte, seated on his other side, engaged his attention more than was strictly polite. Unable to hear her cousin's words, she could only hope that the girl remembered she was a guest in the house.

On Richard's other side, Madame Juliette was entertaining Lady Malden, Emily and George with tales of the theatre, while Lady Grey continued to laud the lady's reputation as a medium whenever she could. Now and again, Richard contrived to touch Maryanne's hand as dinner progressed, making sure she was never without conversation; an unnecessary but courteous attention.

When Mr Taylor turned his charming attention to her at last, Maryanne recognised again the man's possible attraction to young ladies, although she sensed an undercurrent of unease about him.

"Have you been to London before, Miss Robertson?" Mr Taylor enquired, his deep-set eyes staring into hers.

"I confess I have not, but there is too much to see in so short a time."

"And do you have a particular interest while here?"

Maryanne considered her answer and decided to be candid.

"I have a great interest in the stars, planets and the night sky and hope to attend a lecture perhaps, although I'm as eager to visit the theatre as my cousins."

"You like astronomy, Miss Robertson? How interesting. If I should hear of a suitable meeting, I shall inform Lady Malden."

"May I ask where your own interest lies, Mr Taylor?"

The briefest of pauses allowed Charlotte's voice to intervene and claim his attention again. Smiling an apology to Maryanne, he turned to speak to her cousin.

Maryanne frowned, not at the interruption, but with the certainty that Mr Taylor had not wished to divulge information about himself for whatever reason. Perhaps she would find out more about him from Charlotte.

The remainder of dinner soon passed in laughter and chatter until Lady Malden stood up.

"Ladies and gentlemen, please join me in the parlour for this evening's entertainment."

Chapter Four

Filled with misgiving at whatever was about to take place, Maryanne took her seat at the round table obviously brought to the room for this purpose. Relieved Richard was beside her, she noticed Emily's discomfort matched her own while, more worryingly, Charlotte had an air of excitement about her.

"I shall hand over proceedings to Madame Juliette and only ask that you please do exactly as she says." Lady Malden took her seat at the opposite end of the table.

Madame addressed the waiting guests. "I must emphasise there is nothing to worry about and to warn you that the spirits do not always visit during a séance."

Hardly reassuring, Maryanne decided, catching Richard's eye. She had an absurd and sudden desire to giggle and turned her gaze on Charlotte to keep her focused, then concentrated on Madame Juliette's instructions. She had only vaguely heard of such things taking place but was aware that séances were increasingly popular in aristocratic circles.

Madame Juliette addressed them again. "We shall dim the lighting and I wish you to take the hand of the person on either side of you, so that we may make a continuous circle. This is very important so please do not break contact."

Just before the lights dimmed, Maryanne noticed

the smirk on Mr Taylor's face as he took Charlotte's hand. She doubted if he took this seriously.

Once the room was almost in darkness, the complete silence unnerved Maryanne again and she felt the light pressure of Richard's hand as he squeezed hers. *Concentrate*, she told herself, so that she might not miss anything that suggested the performance was merely for their entertainment and should not be taken too seriously. Yet, she could not shake that memory of the otherworldly presence at Mulberry Manor over a year ago.

Her musings came to an abrupt end when Madame Juliette began to speak, for it was not her usual voice and Maryanne's skin chilled.

"Is there someone here whose name begins with the letter C?" the deep voice asked.

Charlotte gasped and answered at once. "Yes."

Maryanne gripped Richard's hand but was unwilling to break the circle, afraid of what that might do to Charlotte. Emily too had gasped but remained silent.

"There is a message for you," the voice continued. "He is waiting to meet you very soon."

"Who is waiting to meet whom?"

Maryanne realised it was she who asked this question before she could stop herself.

No one answered her question as Madame Juliette began to moan softly.

"There is sadness in this room for one who is lost, but he will…" the voice hesitated as though unwilling to speak more. Then Madame Juliette gasped out, "he will… restore the troubled mind..." before collapsing back on her chair.

"But what does it mean?"

Charlotte had broken the circle and half stood, hand on heart as the candles flickered and lit up the room once more.

"It would seem to be a special message for you, my dear," Lady Grey said to Charlotte. "Sometimes, the spirit guides relay messages from the living as well as the dead."

The alarm on Emily's face echoed that in Maryanne's heart. How could they allow this to happen on Charlotte's very first outing, her first evening away from the manor? Yet it was not of their doing, and Lady Grey was only adding to the confusion.

Richard was beside Charlotte before Maryanne collected herself enough to move.

"Come, Charlotte, perhaps you should retire to your room now."

But Charlotte merely stared at him before answering firmly. "No, thank you. I am perfectly well and wish to stay amongst you all."

Lady Malden, although visibly shaken, took command. "Let us retire to the drawing room ladies and I shall order a little cordial to settle us. You may join us shortly, gentlemen. Allow me to take your arm, Madame Juliette, until you fully recover."

Making certain that Emily was looking after Charlotte, Maryanne glanced at Mr Taylor to find nothing but amusement on his handsome face. Catching her glance, he sketched a mocking bow.

"A most entertaining evening, was it not, Miss Robertson? I confess my scepticism has been challenged."

"I am surprised to hear it, Mr Taylor. I expect it had no importance but merely disturbed my cousin because of the first initial of her name. Please excuse me."

Odious man, seeming to take delight in another's distress. Richard was speaking to George who looked bemused by it all and she left them to their port and conversation while she followed the ladies.

Once in the other room, Lady Malden spoke quietly to Charlotte, making no fuss but ascertaining the girl's state of mind. Madame Juliette was fanning herself in between trying to find out exactly what had happened.

"Have you no recollection of the words you spoke?" Maryanne asked with genuine interest.

"None at all. I am afraid that is how it usually happens. The spirit speaks through me and I am merely a conduit. But I'm sorry if I have caused distress."

"Please don't be concerned, Madame Juliette." Charlotte's voice sounded stronger, all trace of upset gone. "I am quite recovered and must apologise that I reacted so foolishly."

Maryanne was not the only person surprised at how quickly the girl had recovered as she seemed less upset than Madame Juliette. Refusing to speak any further about what had happened, Charlotte accepted the offered drink and proceeded to change the subject to more general talk about London.

When the gentlemen joined them, Maryanne noticed how eagerly Charlotte began conversing with Mr Taylor, which only served to puzzle her and caused even more concern. She knew some relief when Madame Juliette and Mr Taylor took their leave soon after, accompanied by Lady Grey.

The atmosphere undeniably lightened but

Charlotte, too, excused herself and would not allow Maryanne or Emily to see her upstairs.

"I have need to lie down now after such excitement but I am perfectly well, Emily." Charlotte refused her sister's arm with a touch of asperity and Maryanne frowned as she watched the girl leave the room.

"You look pensive, my love," Richard said at her ear.

Maryanne turned to him, replacing the frown with a smile. Emily and George were speaking with Lady Malden so it afforded them a little time for each other.

"I confess my cousin continues to puzzle and worry me in equal measure."

"Charlotte is certainly not as open as Emily, nor as wise as you, but I cannot imagine you need to be her nursemaid. Don't let her spoil your stay here."

"You are quite right. Let's forget about her for a while and tell me what you thought of Madame Juliette and her entertainment."

Maryanne was always grateful for Richard's down to earth sense so was a little taken aback when he frowned.

"I confess I'd thought to find it all a sham, but she seemed genuine enough. I'm interested in Mr Taylor, however, and wonder if he always accompanies the lady. There is something not quite trustworthy about him and his obvious attention to Charlotte."

Before Maryanne could question him further, Lady Malden stood.

"Well, my dears, it is time for me to retire and for the young gentlemen to take their departure. I bid you all goodnight."

Richard and George bowed as the lady left the

room, before George took his farewell of Emily.

"A not so veiled hint that we should not outstay our welcome and be left alone with two such lovely ladies," Richard said, taking Maryanne's hands.

"Truly, I'd rather know you were safely returned to your lodgings at this time of night." Maryanne had heard enough tales of London streets.

Richard laughed before kissing each of her hands. "We know which areas to avoid, my love, so please don't worry yourself over us. Perhaps we could call on you tomorrow for a walk in one of the parks."

"I look forward to it. Goodnight, Richard."

Maryanne hesitated until he drew her into his arms and kissed her soundly, much to her delight.

"Goodnight, my love."

Maryanne and Emily stood together at the window until the men had disappeared from sight.

"Oh, Maryanne, it's so good to see them again, is it not?" Emily rested her head against Maryanne's shoulder as she sighed with pleasure.

"It is indeed, dear cousin."

Before leaving the drawing room, Maryanne held Emily back for a moment.

"I think we need to keep an even closer eye on Charlotte than we realised, Emily."

Emily's large eyes looked frightened and worried. "I wish Madame Juliette had not been here this evening, and I confess to an instant dislike of Mr Taylor, yet Charlotte seemed to find him interesting."

When they retired to their bedrooms, Maryanne lay thinking over the evening, trying to focus on seeing her beloved again rather than the events of the séance. It was an unsettling start to their time in London and she hoped they need not see Mr Taylor again, or Madame Juliette.

As her eyes were finally closing, she sat up again remembering her earlier disquiet. Charlotte had come to London with the intention of meeting someone with whom she had been corresponding. Could that person be Mr Taylor?

Chapter Five

All three young ladies were dressed and eager to be abroad in the city when Richard and George called for them. Even Charlotte had expressed some excitement at taking a walk, much to Maryanne's relief.

When they reached Hyde Park, they soon joined the throng of people taking advantage of a fine day, including several black-clad nannies pushing a perambulator or enjoying a seat while their tiny charges slept. One or two older children whooped as they ran along a path trying to keep a hoop circling, often chided whenever they veered too near a couple walking.

A few riders made use of Rotten Row and Maryanne smiled at the elegant picture they made on their high horses.

"Do you ride often, Richard?" she asked at one point, realising she still had much to find out about him.

"Not as often as I'd like. It's easier when I'm at Carmichael Hall, of course, when I take full advantage of being in the countryside. Do you ride, Maryanne?"

"I fear not. There was never a convenient horse for my use, although I should not mind trying if ever I have the opportunity."

"Then I shall make certain to teach you one day," he said and Maryanne's happiness soared.

Emily, George and Charlotte walked a little ahead

and Maryanne wished she could delay their return to the house so she might enjoy Richard's company for as long as possible.

They had almost reached the end of the path when Maryanne's attention was caught by a man coming towards them and she faltered, recognising him too clearly.

"Good morning, ladies, gentlemen. I trust you're well this fine day."

"Mr Taylor. Good morning." Charlotte was the first to answer.

Maryanne forced a smile and noticed Emily barely glanced at him, keeping her hand on George's arm.

Richard and George both acknowledged the man but did not invite further conversation.

Charlotte obviously had other ideas. "Please do take a walk with us, Mr Taylor, if you are not otherwise engaged."

"That would be most pleasant. Thank you, Miss Harrington. May I offer you my arm?"

Neither Maryanne nor Emily could intervene without good cause, or making a fuss, but Maryanne was unhappy that Mr Taylor had happened upon them so conveniently. She tried to remember if he had heard them arranging a walk or if he had departed by then.

"Am I correct in thinking the man is taken with Charlotte, and that your scowl means you disapprove, Maryanne?" Richard regained her attention.

Unaware she had given herself away so thoroughly, Maryanne took Richard's arm again as they walked behind the other two couples.

"It is a little convenient, is it not, that he's here at the exact time we are?"

"It may very well be nothing more than coincidence, of course," Richard said.

Maryanne nodded but was not convinced. For some reason, she was quite certain this meeting had been arranged, or enabled by Mr Taylor.

By the time they had strolled twice around the park, Maryanne agreed it was time to return to Lady Malden. An invitation to a soirée had been confirmed for the evening and they were to take tea with some of Lady Malden's friends during the afternoon. She was pleased that Richard and George had also been invited in the evening.

Before leaving the park, Mr Taylor bid them farewell, bowing over Charlotte's hand a little too closely. "I do hope I may have the pleasure of your company on another occasion very soon."

He straightened to take his leave of the others, reserving his amused half smile for Maryanne, as though he was perfectly aware of her disapproval.

But she had the strongest feeling he had whispered something else to Charlotte before turning to them. Surely he was not arranging a clandestine meeting with her cousin?

Since Charlotte was in good spirits on their approach to Lady Malden's, Maryanne ignored her misgivings for now. Perhaps the girl was merely pleased to have the attention of a handsome man, since it could not be easy being with two couples who were obviously in love. That thought caused her a pang of guilt and she determined to include Charlotte in everything as far as possible so that she may not feel excluded. Perhaps a shopping trip for the ladies would be the very thing, without any gentlemen to distract the pleasure of choosing trinkets.

She suggested it over the light lunch with Lady Malden.

"Why, that is an excellent idea, Maryanne. You must not return home without visiting some of our famous shops, even if you do not wish to purchase much."

Emily was equally excited, as she tended to be about everything, and even Charlotte smiled in agreement.

"Then it is settled. We shall go in the morning after breakfast when we are fresh. Now I suggest a short rest, as we have a busy afternoon and evening ahead."

The afternoon tea was held at a nearby town house of Lady Malden's friend, Mrs Worthington, allowing the ladies to enjoy a short stroll. The sun had strengthened since morning, proving to be the kind of late summery day that brought unexpected warmth. Maryanne reflected that autumn would already be approaching further north.

The lady who welcomed them to her home was a little younger than Lady Malden, her husband seemingly a valued member of parliament. Maryanne was pleased to find Lady Grey in attendance again, who proved as friendly as before, introducing Maryanne and her cousins to some of the other ladies.

Mrs Worthington's two daughters were around their own age and greeted them with curiosity and delight at meeting new young guests.

"You must find London dull at the moment," Hortense, the elder of the two said, eyeing them up and down as though inspecting their manner of dress.

"Not at all," Maryanne assured her. "It is far more exciting than where we live."

Emily agreed at once. "I confess I've never been anywhere as wondrous in my life!"

So far, Charlotte had been content to listen half-heartedly, her thoughts obviously elsewhere. But a comment from the younger Worthington girl, Elizabeth, aroused her attention.

"Mama told us you had a visit from the famous spiritualist," Elizabeth said.

Maryanne confirmed it was true, hoping to change the subject but the girl would not be distracted.

"I believe she received a message for someone. How wonderful, and a little terrifying!"

Maryanne fervently hoped she did not know it was for Charlotte and was relieved when a footman brought in the silver tea urn and delicate porcelain cups and saucers. The trays of small savoury tarts, sweet pastries and tiny cakes soon silenced the chattering while each partook of the tempting delicacies.

However, it soon became evident that Lady Grey had caught mention of Madame Juliette and most of the ladies were happy to share what they knew or had heard.

"She allowed my dearest Mama to tell me she was happy on the other side," one lady said.

"And she told me I would not always be alone," another rather plain lady confirmed.

In the midst of the ensuing gossip, Maryanne noticed that Charlotte listened very carefully to everyone but declined to enter the conversation until Mr Taylor was mentioned.

"Have you met the young gentleman that often

accompanies her?" Elizabeth asked Maryanne and her cousins. "Isn't he handsome?"

"Although a little arrogant for my taste," Hortense said, eliciting a sigh from her sister. "And I did hear a whisper that he is not quite to be trusted around innocent young ladies."

"Pah! Hortense thinks all young men arrogant, with dishonourable intentions. She is hoping for an older husband to keep her in riches," Elizabeth said with a touch of derision.

Reflecting that neither sister was uncommonly handsome, Maryanne kept silent at the exchange, glad she had already met her future husband. But that was an interesting snippet about Mr Taylor's reputation, and her every instinct suspected there may be some truth to it.

Charlotte suddenly entered the conversation. "We *have* met Mr Taylor. He is a most charming man."

Both Worthington girls looked at her with interest. "You have spoken with him?" Elizabeth asked.

"Why, yes," Charlotte replied. "In fact, we were in his company only this morning at the park. He walked part of the way with me and we enjoyed a conversation together."

"Oh, how lovely." Elizabeth looked most envious and seemed at a loss for any further words.

Maryanne had the sudden suspicion that Charlotte was satisfied with that response, yet had not thought her so unkind as to deliberately cause envy in another. Did she then hope to further her acquaintance with Mr Taylor?

"We do not know much about the gentleman, however. It was a happy coincidence that he was taking a stroll at the same time," Maryanne reassured Elizabeth.

Charlotte appeared bored with the conversation and sipped her tea while Emily accepted another pastry from Hortense.

There was no further mention of Madame Juliette or Mr Taylor, as Lady Malden ensured her young charges met each of the ladies in the room before it was an acceptable time to leave. But the conversation lingered in Maryanne's mind long after they had returned home to rest for the evening's outing.

Chapter Six

Tired after such a busy day, Maryanne was happy to spend some time alone before dressing for the evening. She had started to make little notes about her stay in London and all the wonderful sights and experiences, for it might be years before she returned. On the other hand, she might very well be in the city with Richard in the future.

She also recorded her thoughts and misgivings surrounding Charlotte, to try and make sense of them. Both Mr Taylor and Madame Juliette aroused a sense of unease in her, yet they had not actually done anything to concern her unduly.

She was aware that the practise of spiritualism and holding séances was becoming ever more popular amongst the higher echelons of society. Even Queen Victoria and Prince Albert had supposedly participated in a séance several years before at their residence, Osborne House, on the Isle of Wight. She also knew, however, that some so-called spiritualists or mediums preyed on the susceptibility of grieving minds and charged well for the privilege.

Then there was the puzzle of mesmerism and the ability of some to obtain a measure of control over another person's mind, such as happened to Charlotte at Mulberry Manor. There was no doubt that her actions and subsequent distress had not been of her own volition. The question remained as to how much those events still affected her and what could be done?

Happy when Emily reminded her it was time to dress for the evening, Maryanne gave herself up to the clever ministrations of Simmons once again and agreed to wear the light green and blue tartan taffeta gown with its modest lace fichu at the low neckline. It reminded her of home yet was suitable for the occasion, and for seeing Richard again.

Although the evening gathering was held at yet another house belonging to one of Lady Malden's many acquaintances, this one was across London and necessitated a carriage ride through the rapidly darkening streets. Maryanne imagined that many of the narrow alleys would be even more unsafe by evening.

It proved to be a much larger establishment than either Lady Malden's or Mrs Worthington's, and soon filled with many ladies and gentlemen of polite society as far as Maryanne could discern. Although there would be no dancing, a pianist and opera singer had been engaged for their entertainment.

Maryanne's pleasure increased when Richard arrived and came straight to her side while his brother greeted Emily. But she was surprised when Mr Taylor appeared and sought Charlotte's company at once, after bowing to them all.

"Good evening, Mr Taylor. We did not expect to have the pleasure of your company this evening," Maryanne said, resolving to be pleasant to the young man.

"I could scarcely resist the opportunity to see you all again," he replied.

His attention, however, was for Charlotte who inclined her head with a smile, as though his presence was not such a surprise to her. Maryanne hid her concern when Mr Taylor took her cousin's arm and led her to another part of the room, ostensibly to introduce her to someone. After all, she and Emily had the Carmichael brothers attending them.

Suggesting to Richard that they mingle in the company, Maryanne took his arm as they spoke to a few people Richard had met before. All the while, she looked for sight of Charlotte. Soon, she noticed her at one side, still beside Mr Taylor, but in conversation with another smaller, older man. By the time, Maryanne and Richard reached their side, the stranger had gone.

When she spoke to Charlotte, Maryanne was concerned at her vagueness, as though she were suddenly unaware of her surroundings. Mr Taylor did nothing to reassure her, when he excused himself and was soon lost from sight. Neither had mentioned the other man.

"I think you should come and sit down with us for a while, Charlotte," Maryanne suggested. "It is a little warm, perhaps, and we can fetch a drink for you before the musical entertainment."

Finding a few seats to one side, Charlotte gratefully sipped the cordial Richard had brought her, but insisted she was only a little tired. Soon, the guests were required to take their seats in the large music room, where Maryanne forgot everything else as she listened to the accomplished pianist and the dulcet tones of the pleasant soprano.

Afterwards, her pleasure was short-lived when it soon became evident that another unexpected guest was amongst them.

Their hostess, Lady Eldritch, clapped for their attention.

"Ladies and gentlemen, we have a special entertainment this evening for any who wish to join us in the parlour. Madame Juliette has agreed to give us a demonstration of her unique gift."

Maryanne heard Charlotte's gasp and was alarmed when the girl stood up at once.

"Oh, I must attend. Please excuse me."

Maryanne watched in astonishment as Charlotte walked towards Lady Eldritch.

"We must go with her, Richard," Maryanne said, but he was already taking her arm.

Following all those guests intrigued enough to enter the parlour, Maryanne and Richard sat down at the large circular table, ensuring Maryanne was next to Charlotte. Emily and George had not joined them but all seats were occupied. Just before the light dimmed, Maryanne caught sight of Mr Taylor sitting beside the man who had been talking to Charlotte. Surely he could have nothing to do with her cousin's strangeness afterwards?

Maryanne had no wish to attend another séance but would not leave Charlotte's side. Besides, she could see for herself if this *performance* was in any way believable.

The lady herself looked much as she had before, her exotic appearance less obvious in the dimmed room, the few flickering candles adding to the hushed, expectant atmosphere.

Madame Juliette began to speak in softened tones, reminding everyone of the need to maintain the circle. Soon, she began to sway and moan. Maryanne wondered if they were being treated to a more theatrical performance due to the increased numbers, and the suggestion this was entertainment for the guests.

Next minute, Madame Juliette sat bolt upright, her gaze fixed unwaveringly ahead. The voice that spoke next was not her own and Maryanne's grip on Richard's hand tightened while her body chilled.

"There is a lady here who tragically lost a daughter to illness. Annabelle has a message for you…"

A thin, childish voice spoke next. "Dear Mama, please don't be sad. I'm happy here…" and the voice faded while Maryanne could hear soft weeping nearby.

The voice issuing from Madame Juliette changed suddenly to a man's deep timbre. "Are you here, Ellen?"

A woman gasped and cried out, "Yes!"

The man's voice continued. "I'll never stop loving you, my dear…"

Maryanne tried to relax her shoulders, hoping this would soon end, unable to quite believe it was real yet equally unable to refute the evidence of her ears.

Then the voice changed again, to a female this time. "He can help you to recover, Charl…" before fading.

Charlotte's hand left hers as she sagged beside Maryanne.

Madame Juliette said no more and, as further light gradually returned, Maryanne saw the lady was slumped in her seat as though exhausted.

Lady Eldritch immediately took charge. "Thank you, ladies and gentlemen, if you will return to the other room, please. Madame Juliette needs a little time to recover but will be quite all right."

Maryanne and Richard ushered Charlotte from the room, but not before Maryanne saw Mr Taylor sit down beside Madame Juliette and take her hand when the lady's eyes opened.

As soon as they were on their own, Maryanne checked that Charlotte was well enough, amazed to find the girl unconcerned.

"I'm quite well, thank you. Please don't fuss," she said.

"But did you not hear Madame Juliette mention you again?" Maryanne asked.

"I expect she was going to say 'Charles', and someone was merely trying to convince him to accept help." Charlotte looked as though she believed her words.

When Maryanne frowned at Richard, he shook his head and she said no more. Thankfully, the evening was almost over and Lady Malden was happy to take her charges home at Maryanne's request.

Since she had not been at the séance, Maryanne briefly told Lady Malden it had upset Charlotte, which was enough of an excuse.

After such a long day, Maryanne was too tired to tell Emily what had happened. There was little point in worrying her without substance. But she did linger a little with Richard as they said goodnight, grateful as always for his presence and good sense in the midst of her concern.

"Perhaps Charlotte was correct and that message was not meant for her?" he suggested.

"Perhaps. But you saw her reaction at the time. Either she is pretending, or she genuinely believes what she says. Not that we're much wiser as to what it all means."

"Try to sleep, my love, since there's not much you can do for now."

Maryanne longed for sleep but the more she tried to blot out her concerns about Charlotte, and thinking over the events of the evening, the more she tossed and turned.

Who was the mysterious man Charlotte and Mr Taylor had been talking to before the séance and why did her cousin react like that to Madame Juliette's final message?

She was quite convinced it had been meant for Charlotte. But from whom and who was the 'he' mentioned?

Chapter Seven

Maryanne could not deny the excitement of strolling past some of the best shops in London the next morning and resolved to take advantage of the opportunity. After a very disturbed sleep with too many thoughts churning around, she was glad to be out in the pleasant morning light.

Fortunately, she had saved a little money and her mother had insisted she take the gift she had managed to put by from thrifty housekeeping.

Although Maryanne had declined to accept it at first, since her parents were far from wealthy and her papa the kindest of parsons to his parishioners, her mother had been firm.

"You have never had this kind of opportunity, my dear, and your father and I must be allowed to give you this gift before you leave our home forever."

It was the closest her mama had alluded to the possibility of a wedding for their only daughter and Maryanne could not refuse. She had, however, ignored her mother's matrimonial hints.

Now, she fully intended buying her parents a little gift as a memento of her holiday, as well as a trinket for herself if possible. The streets were busy with all types of humanity, including the distressing sight of small ragged urchins narrowly escaping injury from a passing horse and carriage. Street sellers called their wares and grand ladies swept the edge of their gowns aside from any who came too near them. The new omnibuses only added to the noise, while the stench from unwashed bodies, sewers and unidentifiable food assailed Maryanne at times.

Although the sweepers tried to keep control of the debris, it was evidently a battle never likely to be won. If this was one of the better shopping areas, Maryanne dreaded to think what other streets might look like. Her heart already saddened for the dirty children, pick pockets and vagabonds.

She was tempted to give a halfpenny to one little girl with ragged clothes, dirty lank hair and large blue eyes.

"No, my dear, you must not even hint at such a thing," Lady Malden took Maryanne's arm. "You would have half the urchins of London upon us and it would make little difference. In fact, it might even cause a fight amongst them."

Understanding the sense of the words, some of Maryanne's pleasure in the outing receded and she reflected that she must be more like her father than she realised. Nevertheless, she winced when their accompanying manservant pushed aside any child who ventured too close.

Soon, however, they were standing before one of the haberdashery shops that immediately drew their attention. Emily could not wait to enter and even Charlotte smiled at the vast selection of items to browse or buy.

Maryanne should find the very thing for her parents and a fine pair of netted gloves for herself perhaps.

"Oh, look at this exquisite fan," Charlotte said from the other end of the counter. "I shall buy this to use while we are in London."

Although it seemed an unnecessary frippery, Maryanne admired its dainty detail and the fine lace at its edges. It was not to her own taste, however, and she wandered over to see what had caught Emily's attention.

"Isn't this the sweetest pin cushion, Maryanne?"

"It is indeed and I think Mama might be delighted with such an item. Is it very expensive, I wonder?" Maryanne didn't mind asking her dearest cousin such a question.

As though his ears were finely attuned to a possible purchase, the owner sidled along to them at once and mentioned a price that was a little above what Maryanne hoped.

Just then, Lady Malden's voice accosted the man.

"Come now, I think you may have mistaken the cost for another item, have you not?"

Obviously recognising quality and no doubt hopeful of further purchases, the man's obsequiousness amused Maryanne as he rushed to answer such a fine lady.

"Forgive me, your ladyship, you are quite correct. I mistook the item for another more costly one."

The revised sum he mentioned suited Maryanne much better and she handed over her money. Since he was being even more helpful to impress Lady Malden, Maryanne chose the most inexpensive pair of blue short netted gloves for herself before they left the shop behind.

"Now I should like to purchase some new stays, and I dare say you young ladies will enjoy the variety on offer at Carter's Wholesale and Retail establishment at Ludgate Hill. He has the very best French muslin, and even the new crinoline watch-spring petticoats that are becoming fashionable."

Maryanne caught Emily's girlish smile at mention of such items. She, too, was curious to see the latest fashions, even if she could not hope to own expensive, unseen items herself.

True to Lady Malden's promise, none of the young ladies had ever seen such an array of undergarments, petticoats and stays and were content merely to admire while Aunt Drusilla, as Maryanne tried to think of her, ordered what she required.

Once finished, Lady Malden suggested a welcome visit to a nearby tearoom, insisting they needed sustenance for more shopping and strolling.

Maryanne raised her eyebrows at the three-tier stand of dainty cakes brought to the table by a pretty young girl with a pristine white apron over her dark gown. A veritable feast to Maryanne's eyes. Delicate China cups and saucers followed, patterned with red and pink roses.

When all had taken their fill, they left the shop eager to walk off their overindulgence. They had no sooner gone in the direction of their next destination when Emily noticed Richard and George coming towards them.

"Good morning, ladies," Richard doffed his hat while George kissed Emily's hand, eliciting a pretty blush on her fair cheeks.

"May we walk a little way with you?" Richard asked, immediately taking his place beside Maryanne.

"You may, until we reach the next shop then you may leave us," Lady Malden said with a smile. "I cannot imagine you would enjoy the types of purchases we are making."

Richard winked at Maryanne and inclined his head to Lady Malden. "I expect you are quite correct, for we have no interest in ladies' fripperies. But may I take Maryanne aside for a moment as I wish to draw her attention to an interest we share."

Maryanne hardly needed her hostess's approval but was pleased Richard had given the lady her place.

"We shall wait for you at the chemist shop further along, Maryanne, for I should like to purchase some scented soap." Lady Malden walked ahead with Emily and Charlotte, still accompanied by George.

"Take my arm if you will, Maryanne, and we shall stroll as we talk," Richard said.

Pleased to enjoy a walk with her beloved rather than enduring the stuffiness of shops, Maryanne took his arm, wondering if there was indeed some news to impart.

"I assume you are still interested in the stars?" Richard asked, glancing into her eyes.

"Yes, indeed, although my knowledge is still sadly lacking."

"I have the ideal suggestion. There is to be a meeting of astronomers this evening and I should like to attend. Perhaps you might accompany me?"

Heart quickening at the thought of an evening out with Richard where she might also learn something, Maryanne smiled up at her handsome escort.

"I should enjoy that immensely. Thank you. However, you must gain Lady Malden's agreement since I am staying with her."

"Then we shall do that as soon as we reach her. I'm

so pleased to see you again, Maryanne, and long for us to make arrangements for our future."

"No more than I do."

Happy that nothing was marring their meeting this time, Maryanne relinquished his arm with reluctance as they approached the others.

Lady Malden had no objection to Maryanne's attendance at a meeting with Richard but issued a stern warning about bringing her home safely. He had no trouble charming the older lady with promises and assurances.

"I shall take Emily and Charlotte to a small evening soirée while you are being bored by science," Lady Malden promised.

Maryanne smiled, knowing full well that the lady was interested in all manner of interesting subjects herself. But it would give her a good opportunity to spend time with her nieces and introduce them to her acquaintances. Maryanne would far rather enjoy a lecture, not least because she would be accompanied by Richard.

But Charlotte had other ideas, it seemed.

"If you will forgive me, Aunt Drusilla, I seem to be getting a headache and would rather stay indoors this evening. But I shall be perfectly happy with my own company and insist you take Emily as planned."

"Oh my dear, we must return home if you are in pain. We are finished here. Perhaps a lie down will restore you for this evening."

"Thank you, Aunt, but please don't rush your outing on my behalf."

"Nonsense. I'm quite certain we shall have another opportunity to visit the shops when you are feeling more rested." Lady Malden had decided.

Maryanne was perfectly content to return to the house, especially since she had made a purchase and had this evening's outing with Richard ahead.

But when she glanced at her cousin, a prickle of unease made her shiver. She suspected that Charlotte's headache was an excuse so that she might be left at home by herself. But for what reason? There was little likelihood that anyone would call on her, or be admitted, when the lady of the house was absent.

It was only when they returned to Lady Malden's, that Maryanne had a terrible suspicion Charlotte would not be at home either this evening. Or was she letting her imagination run away with her? Perhaps her cousin merely wished to avoid the somewhat tiring round of social events after being enclosed at Mulberry Manor for so long. Maryanne could only pray that the girl would not be so foolish as to risk an outing in London at night without a proper, and safe, escort.

Chapter Eight

Maryanne had to admit she was excited to be dressing for another evening out. Less formal than a ball, she still had the opportunity to wear one of her favourite gowns that befitted the city.

Simmons was equally happy to help her to dress and to arrange her hair in a more elaborate style but one that would remain in place for the whole evening.

"Remember I am only going to a meeting place and not to a fancy ball, please," she told the eager young maid.

Her gentle admonition went unheeded as her thick hair was twisted into a becoming shape on the back of her head, allowing a single curl to fall at either side of her face.

The crinoline they had chosen was dark green with cream lace at the neck and edge of sleeves. Pretty but not too ostentatious nor too low at the front. Simmons fastened a single pearl necklet around Maryanne's throat to match the small earrings. Her warmer cloak should suffice for the journey there.

Lady Malden and Emily gave their approval when she eventually came downstairs. Both of them were already gowned and coiffed for their own evening out, but Charlotte had obviously kept to her room. Perhaps she really did have the headache.

Richard arrived exactly on time and had to listen again to Lady Malden's homily on his responsibility for Maryanne's safety.

"I will guard her with my life, Lady Malden."

Although Maryanne was delighted with his response, Lady Malden flicked her closed fan at him.

"One would hope such drama will be unnecessary. It will suffice that you bring Maryanne home intact."

Aware of the warmth creeping up her face at such an ambiguous warning, Maryanne caught Richard's grin before he gave a half bow to the lady with promises to be on his best behaviour. Even Emily was smiling at the exchange.

Gladly taking his arm, Maryanne was relieved when they departed the house before Lady Malden offered any further advice. Since the meeting place was not too far away, they had decided to walk on such a fine evening.

"Thank you for not insisting on a carriage, Maryanne. I confess I miss the countryside when in London and enjoy any excuse for some exercise." He tucked her hand in the crook of his elbow.

"I completely agree and look forward to exploring more of the wonderful parks nearby." Maryanne glanced up at him, pleased to be anywhere in his company.

The streets were busy with all manner of people either strolling like them or hurrying down some of the dark alleys here and there. Carriages conveyed the well-to-do while a few street urchins still lurked in the shadows hoping to earn a coin or a crust by fair means or foul.

Richard had already warned her about pickpockets and she stayed close to his side, lest one of the poorer ragged men accosted them. Now and then, she spotted a police constable which reassured her a little. Yet it was exciting to be walking through the evening streets of London where only the lamplight illuminated their way. At least the dreaded pea soup fog was absent for now, which allowed fair visibility.

When they reached the meeting room, Maryanne was gratified to see she was not the only female who had come to hear about the latest astronomical discoveries, although they were far outnumbered by the men.

As they took their seats at the end of a row, she glanced around at the building and the audience, appreciating the fine corniced ceiling. Her attention was soon brought to the front again when a man addressed them from the small stage.

"Good evening… ladies, and gentlemen."

Maryanne was not the only one to appreciate his hesitation at seeing the audience not composed only of men and she smiled at Richard, thankful he understood and encouraged her curiosity.

"We have a special guest for your enjoyment tonight so please welcome Mr Charles Morrison. We are most privileged that he will include the most recent information about the comet seen in parts of Europe."

Maryanne was soon enthralled with the talk about the solar system, not least because she was in the fine company of so many others interested in the subject.

"And the most exciting event to be reported over the past few months was the discovery of a comet which is large and brilliant enough to be visible to the eye," Mr Morrison told them proudly, as though he personally had arranged it for them.

"It may interest you to know that the closest it has

come to earth thus far was on the 11th of July," he added, and looked gratified at the gasps of amazement.

"Will it come closer, d'you think?" asked one man with an extravagant moustache.

"We do not think so, but one never knows exactly what might happen in our infinite skies."

A few of the audience agreed, while Maryanne shared Richard's smile at such a non-committal answer, however true it might be. No matter what else they attended while in London, Maryanne decided, this would be one of her most treasured visits.

The streets had darkened even more when they took their leave at the end. Maryanne was thankful for Richard's tall physical presence beside her, his top hat adding even more inches. Taking his arm with pride, she smiled up at him whenever he asked a question or discussed the evening's meeting.

"I think this is one of my happiest outings, Richard," she said at one point.

"I confess you greatly add to my happiness by being here beside me, my love."

Content to prolong their evening, they strolled alongside one of the parks, away from the main crush of other people leaving a theatre or music hall.

As they turned a corner, a familiar sounding voice caught Maryanne's attention and she paused.

"What is it, Maryanne? Is something wrong?"

Maryanne pressed a finger to her lips as she tried to hear the conversation nearby, although the voices were lowered so that she struggled to know if she had heard correctly.

Turning her face away, she whispered to Richard.

"I think that's Charlotte's voice. It sounds like

she's speaking to someone, although she is supposed to be at home with a headache." *Could it be Mr Taylor?*

"Are you quite sure?"

Maryanne listened another moment and was increasingly convinced she was right.

"Can we wait to see what happens, please? I must ensure she is unharmed and returns home safely. Whatever she is doing, I would never forgive myself if anything were to happen to her."

Although she spoke the truth, Maryanne was angry that Charlotte had been so foolish to sneak out of the house by herself in such a large city, never mind her dishonest subterfuge while a guest of Lady Malden.

They did not have long to wait when the other person loped away through the darkness before Maryanne could see him properly. For it was certainly a man, placing Charlotte in even more possible danger in so many ways.

As soon as the girl started towards them, Maryanne stepped out of the shadows and was momentarily pleased to see the fear on her cousin's face until she identified them.

"Oh, Maryanne! And Richard. You startled me."

"I am very glad of it, for we might have been anyone ready to accost you, cousin. How come you to be abroad in the dark by yourself?" Maryanne did nothing to hide her anger.

"My headache was a little better and I had need of some air after being confined in my room."

Maryanne had to applaud the girl's calmness, although she obviously had no intention of mentioning whoever she had met.

"Did we not hear you in conversation just now?"

Maryanne asked.

Charlotte looked around as though to make sure no one was in sight. "Someone asked for directions, but I could not help and didn't want to linger here."

Maryanne glanced at Richard, unsure how to accuse her cousin of lying.

"It certainly sounded more like a conversation," he said, "from the little we heard."

"You are quite mistaken. Now may we please go home, for I feel another headache coming on." Charlotte walked straight ahead, forcing Maryanne and Richard to follow.

Disappointed that Charlotte could lie so convincingly, Maryanne hoped she might find a way to gain the girl's confidence before she did meet with an accident or worse.

Fortunately, Lady Malden and Emily were not yet home and Charlotte went straight to her room while Maryanne said goodnight to Richard.

"Thank you for a wonderful evening," she said. "It has added so much to my knowledge, if I can recall even half of the information."

"Perhaps we'll find a good pamphlet on the subject from one of the many book shops in London. Meanwhile, have a restful sleep and try not to worry too much about your errant cousin. I shall call upon you tomorrow and we have the theatre visit in the evening."

"Another delightful treat. Goodnight, Richard."

Standing on tiptoe to accept his kiss, Maryanne wished they had not met Charlotte and might have lingered a little longer on the way home.

Once upstairs, she was determined to speak to her

cousin, else she would not sleep soundly. Knocking lightly on the bedroom door, she heard Charlotte's voice bid her enter.

Surprised at gaining entry so easily, Maryanne saw the girl was agitated and still in her gown so obviously had not yet called for the maid.

She went to Maryanne immediately. "Promise me you will not mention my walk to anyone, cousin," she entreated.

Maryanne noticed the wildness in the dark blue eyes and was concerned at the girl's restlessness.

"Come and sit down, Charlotte, and tell me what is going on. I cannot make any promises without knowing what you're involved in."

Obviously reluctant to comply, Charlotte finally sat on the edge of her bed, hands twisting together, hesitating for so long that Maryanne wondered if she would speak at all.

"If I confide in you a little, you must not tell Emily or Lady Malden."

Maryanne inclined her head, unwilling to promise words she might regret.

"I was not completely alone this evening. Mr Taylor accompanied me but hid in the shadows to wait until my meeting was over."

Charlotte's eyes had calmed a little but her hands were still agitated and Maryanne allowed her to continue without comment, although she was alarmed at the thought of her cousin meeting someone without their knowledge.

"Mr Taylor must have seen you and Richard and knew I would reach home safely."

"But whom were you meeting, Charlotte?"

Maryanne could wait no longer.

Again, the hesitation and Maryanne held her breath.

"The person with whom I've been corresponding these past months. Oh, please do not ask me any more for I promised to keep it a secret, lest it be misunderstood."

Maryanne took the girl's hands, to still them apart from anything else. Surely her cousin could not imagine she would leave it there?

"Listen to me, Charlotte. You must know it's impossible that I turn away from such revelations and allow you to possibly put yourself in danger."

Charlotte removed her hands from Maryanne's. "I shall not be stopped from what I came here to do, Maryanne. And Mr Taylor has kindly agreed to escort me when necessary so I shall not be alone."

Alarmed now at her cousin's change of manner and tone, Maryanne stood up. She was scarcely reassured at mention of Mr Taylor's attention since that man was possibly not to be trusted, although only her inner feelings, and that fragment of gossip, told her so.

"I shall let you rest now, Charlotte, but I'm determined to know more and can only plead that you'll not do anything foolish, dangerous, or that might tarnish your reputation."

Charlotte also stood, her shoulders relaxing now that the questioning was over.

"Thank you, Maryanne. You are kind to be so concerned and I will be careful, although I no longer care about my reputation since it was already tarnished after the events at Mulberry Manor, if you recall."

Maryanne turned back from the door. "That is

untrue, Charlotte. None of what happened was your fault. And please think of your sister's good name if not your own."

"Goodnight, Maryanne." Charlotte held the door open.

"Sleep well, Charlotte."

Maryanne was relieved to seek refuge in her own bedroom before there was any chance of Emily returning to tell her about her evening.

The pleasure in her own evening out with Richard was reduced by worry about her cousin. Although she still had no idea what or who the girl was involved with, Maryanne was determined to find out very soon.

Chapter Nine

The following day, their excited chatter was all about that evening's visit to the theatre. Emily could talk of nothing else and was already planning her outfit.

"We shall have the better seats of course," Lady Malden said. "I'm afraid you will find all manner of people crowded together at certain places. And I must warn you that they may not keep quiet."

"It sounds very interesting," Maryanne said, grateful to have this opportunity to visit one of the famous London theatres, no matter who was there or how noisy it might be.

"It is certainly that, my dear. Now I suggest a walk in the park, followed by a short visit to Sangster's to look at their new parasols. That should occupy you all for some of the day at least."

Before they departed for their walk, however, Richard arrived with some exciting news.

"If you will permit me to interfere with any plans you may have for tomorrow, Lady Malden, I have an invitation."

"Pray sit down and acquaint us with your news, Mr Carmichael." Lady Malden arranged herself on the high-backed chair while Maryanne and her cousins sat on the sofa.

Maryanne smiled at her beloved and knew whatever he had planned would no doubt please her.

"I have obtained tickets to the Crystal Palace and

thought the young ladies might not have another opportunity to see such wonders. Although it is not quite as magnificent as the Great Exhibition of 1851, it is still a place of marvels."

Maryanne gasped in delight. "Oh, Lady Malden, I should like that very much indeed."

The lady glanced at her in surprise before addressing Richard.

"It would seem that at least one young lady is almost overcome at such a notion. As it happens, I have had the pleasure of visiting it myself and I think it would be a most admirable outing. Thank you, young man."

Maryanne's racing heartbeat slowed a little once she knew they were allowed to visit the one place she had dreamed of when first hearing of its opening some years ago. She glanced at Emily and Charlotte who had remained quiet, but at least Emily was smiling in agreement.

"Shall George accompany us?" Emily asked, and on receiving the affirmative, she smiled even wider.

Maryanne suspected that Emily would agree to anything as long as George was by her side. Charlotte's countenance was carefully devoid of any emotion, whether pleasure or distaste. Rather she seemed completely indifferent to their discussion, her gaze moving to the large window now and then. Searching for someone, perhaps?

"I look forward to escorting all of you lovely ladies to the theatre this evening, but for now I bid you farewell." Richard replaced his top hat and Maryanne walked to the door with him.

"Thank you for arranging our visit to a place I've

longed to see, Richard." Maryanne touched his arm.

"Anything for you, my love." And he gave her a fleeting kiss before taking his leave.

Maryanne stood for a moment to compose herself before returning to the others, aware of the heat most likely staining her cheeks.

Emily and Charlotte had already gone upstairs to dress for the outing to the park and Lady Malden smiled knowingly at Maryanne.

"I think he is a most suitable young man, my dear, and I trust it will not be too long before you are together." To save Maryanne replying, she continued, "now run along and fetch your coat and hat for our walk in the park."

Glad to be dismissed, Maryanne did as directed and was soon ready to leave with her cousins. It was such a pleasant morning that she looked forward to a stroll in the open air.

The park was busy with other people taking the air and once again Maryanne marvelled at the variety of ladies and gentlemen in their finery, parasols protecting the ladies' faces.

Although Charlotte had agreed to accompany them, she refused to enter into the general chatter and strolled along just behind them. Maryanne checked now and then that she was still there but soon gave up any pretence of trying to engage her cousin in conversation.

They were nearing a small boating pond when a sudden cry alerted them to someone in trouble and they hurried in the direction of the shrieks. A young woman stood clutching at her chest and pointing to the water.

When they reached her side, Maryanne saw a small

child obviously in trouble even though the water was not very deep. About to rush in to fetch the child, she paused when a young man came running to the pond and strode straight in.

The woman stopped screaming and Maryanne tried to comfort her while they watched the man carry the child in his arms. Laying him on the ground, he gently tapped the boy's cheeks and moved him onto his front to try and dislodge any water.

It was only then that Maryanne recognised Mr Taylor.

Next minute the boy coughed and spluttered and managed to sit up.

"Oh, my little Edward, I thought I'd lost you." The mother sobbed as she grasped the child to her bosom and rocked him back and forth.

When he appeared to recover a little more, she stood up and held out her hand to Mr Taylor.

"I cannot thank you enough, sir. You have saved my boy."

"I'm only glad I was nearby. He should be well enough after a good rest, and warm dry clothes."

It struck Maryanne that the man knew what he was talking about and she wondered again about his private life. But Charlotte distracted her by going straight to Mr Taylor.

"How very good of you to rescue the little boy, Mr Taylor. It's a pleasure to meet you here again. But you are also in need of dry shoes."

"Miss Harrington. The pleasure is mine and the boy only required someone to lift him to safety. My feet scarcely touched the water for long. May I walk with you?"

Receiving a nod from Lady Malden, who had watched everything without comment, Charlotte took Mr Taylor's arm as they all proceeded on their stroll.

Maryanne noticed the colour in Charlotte's cheeks, her whole countenance now more animated, and surmised that Mr Taylor must be the reason. She must enlist Richard's help to try and find out more about the gentleman before her cousin became any further enamoured. Yet, she could not dismiss the fact that Charlotte had been corresponding with someone else. How confusing the girl had become.

The remainder of the stroll passed uneventfully and they said goodbye to Mr Taylor before continuing to some of the better shops. Maryanne happened to look towards Charlotte as he took his leave and was certain that her cousin had handed a piece of paper to the gentleman, which he hastily pushed inside his pocket. As soon as he had gone, Charlotte once more retreated to near silence and her own thoughts.

The visit to W & J Sangster in Regent Street helped to distract her concern, for the moment at least, but she kept a close eye on Charlotte. While Lady Malden purchased a beautiful parasol in China crape, Maryanne was pleased to see her cousin show some interest in the variety of items in brocades and Irish lace.

But all the while, Maryanne was mindful of that scrap of paper and even more troubled at what mischief her cousin might be involved in. Thankfully, they were all going to the theatre that evening and her excitement at visiting the Crystal Palace the day after was enough to distract her worrying any further about her cousin for now.

Chapter Ten

Maryanne shared Emily's excitement as they dressed for the evening at the Adelphi Theatre. Even the name sounded exotic and exciting, never mind the play they were about to enjoy, although Maryanne surmised that viewing the other people in the audience would be as much of an entertainment as the actors on stage. Richard had explained that the current theatre was in fact the third, having been rebuilt as recently as 1858.

They arrived in a carriage that jostled for space with the many others delivering their occupants as near to the theatre as possible and Maryanne was overwhelmed for a moment by the numbers entering. Soon, however, she was entertained by the variety of people and modes of dress. Once inside, it was the plush surroundings that captured her attention, even more lavish when they took their privileged seats.

In addition to the stalls, three tiers of curved balconied seats rose up into the heights, every one seemingly occupied. A private box was situated at the stage side of each tier, one of which she was delighted to find awaiting their party. Maryanne stared at the plush velvet curtain currently closed across the stage and could only imagine the excitement behind the screen.

All around, the buzz of voices created a volume of noise that Maryanne was unused to but it was good natured, tinged with excitement. She wondered how many other people were visiting the theatre for the first time.

She was most pleased that Richard was seated beside her, and breathed in his masculine scent.

"Hopefully, some of the rowdier elements will calm down a little when it begins," he whispered. "This type of burlesque drama is popular with a more literate audience and is rather an extravaganza at times, so don't take it too seriously."

Maryanne glanced at the several men and women standing to the front of the auditorium who were already in high spirits.

"It adds to the fun," she said, hoping they would indeed be a little quieter so she might hear the play they had come to watch.

She glanced around as far as she was able, pleased to find all the seats taken. Two boxes across from them were also occupied and she smiled to see the ladies dressed much like themselves. These more costly seats allowed a modicum of privacy as well as an excellent view of the stage.

Quite suddenly, her gaze alighted on a man who seemed somewhat familiar, although she could not place him. Not Mr Taylor however. This man seemed taller, more subdued than the flamboyant gentleman of their acquaintance.

Maryanne's face warmed when the man glanced her way, yet she was aware it was not she who held his attention. Quickly fanning her face, Maryanne turned slightly and found the focus of his gaze.

Charlotte was staring straight at the man, a pretty blush on her face, her fan concealing her mouth and chin. Aware of Maryanne's interest, Charlotte turned her attention to the stage just as the curtain began to open.

Maryanne frowned as she tried to think where she might have seen the man before. There was too great a distance to be certain of his features but she was convinced she had met him, although not recently.

The beginning of the play commanded her concentration and she pushed the puzzle away to be mused over later. Titled *The Enchanted Isle*, it was seemingly based on Shakespeare's *The Tempest*. Soon, she completely forgot about everything and everyone else as she became involved in the amusing burlesque type drama taking place on stage. The costumes, the music, the comic rhyming lines delivered by commanding actors, and the pretty dancer in her frilled dress all captured her attention.

At one scene, she discovered her hand gripping Richard's but before she could remove it, he covered it with his own and they remained that way until the end.

It was only at the final act of the play that Maryanne remembered the man who had been staring their way. She resolved to keep an eye on Charlotte when it ended, but there was such a surge of people trying to find the exit that it was only by staying close to Richard she was prevented from being separated from the rest of their party.

"Keep close by my side, Maryanne," Richard said in her ear. "It is a little unruly at the end of a performance."

Happy to take his arm as she was caught in the melee, Maryanne reassured herself that Emily was safely by George while Lady Malden was more than capable of forging a passage through to the exit. The only person she could not see was Charlotte.

Hesitating, while looking behind them, Maryanne found it impossible to stop or she risked being separated from Richard and could only hope her cousin was already at the exit or waiting outside.

Relieved to finally feel the cool night air on her face, Maryanne smiled to see Emily, George and Lady Malden waiting outside. Of Charlotte, however, there was no sign.

Chapter Eleven

"Where is my sister? Emily looked around and beyond Maryanne as though expecting to see her materialise. "I assumed Charlotte was with you."

"And we hoped you were all together," Maryanne said.

As panic threatened to disrupt the evening, Lady Malden's voice drew their attention.

"I do believe my niece has found us. Here she is now."

Maryanne turned to see Charlotte almost upon them, unaccompanied as far as she could discern.

"Where have you been?" Emily cried, embracing her sister. "We thought you lost."

"I seemed to be carried along in a different direction for a time, but I'm here now and there is no need to scold, Emily." Charlotte frowned at her sister before turning to Lady Malden. "I apologise for keeping you waiting, Aunt Drusilla."

"Well, no harm done, child, but let us make our way home."

Maryanne glanced around once more, seeking any sign of the gentleman she had noticed in the other box but most people had already vacated the theatre and she saw no one recognisable. She was quite certain, however, that Charlotte had deliberately stepped away from them at some point. To meet someone, perhaps?

Richard took her arm as he spoke for her ears only.

"I suspect your cousin is not quite as innocent as she pretends."

Maryanne was unsurprised at his observation and agreed. "I fear she'll lead us more of a merry dance before we leave London, although I'm determined to discover her mysterious correspondent. No doubt she is arranging every opportunity to meet whoever it is and I must be ready."

"*We* shall be ready for whatever happens, if you'll permit, for I should not like to think of *you* getting into trouble." Richard smiled to allay any suggestion of interference.

"While I have no intention of looking for trouble, you're most welcome to join me whenever possible." Maryanne had every intention of seeking his company when she could and her heart warmed at his agreement.

Once the ladies were safely delivered home, Richard and George took their leave, assuring them they looked forward to their visit to the Crystal Palace with as much enjoyment as anyone else.

Maryanne could scarcely contain her excitement at visiting the 'Palace of the People' at last, as she had heard it named. Richard told them a little of what to expect.

"I suspect you'll find it rather overwhelming at first, ladies," he warned them.

"What kind of things might we see?" Maryanne asked.

"In addition to exhibitions on everything from flowers, animals and birds to transport and myriad other wonders, there are often shows and even massed bands at certain times."

"How exciting," Emily said, eyes shining. "I do

hope we see as much as possible."

George grinned at her before adding, "Watch out for the male statues, draped for modesty. I'm afraid some people objected to the fig leaves."

Emily's face coloured as Maryanne laughed and replied. "I'm certain we'll find better amusement to capture our interest, George."

Richard added another point of interest. "If we're fortunate, we might hear a musical concert. There are over four thousand seats in the concert room and a magnificent Grand Organ in the transept."

"And don't forget all the meetings that take place," George added.

Charlotte had been silent until then, but now asked a question. "What manner of meetings?"

"Oh, various sorts, I've heard. Such as the Temperance League and Salvation Army as well as many organisations and societies."

Charlotte merely nodded and Maryanne wondered why the girl was so interested in this above any other. Then she recalled Charlotte mentioning her hope to attend a certain type of meeting while in London. Did she hope to find one at such a venue?

The more she had heard, the more Maryanne longed to be there. She had gleaned only the merest information about the palace but nothing could compare with the reality of being in its midst. She remembered one interesting detail.

"Is it true there are sometimes circuses and pantomimes?" she asked.

"I believe so," Richard said. "Though I should imagine they'll only be at specific times."

Maryanne suddenly recalled the mummers who

had arrived at Carmichael Hall last Christmas and the subsequent events. It also reminded her about her cousin Henry. He had conducted himself very well in helping the girl with whom he had formed a subsequent attachment.

She asked Emily and Charlotte about their brother. "I meant to ask after Henry. Is he well?"

"Very well indeed," Emily said. "In fact, I rather think he and Felicity King are to be married next year, although nothing definite has been arranged. Isn't that wonderful? Little Harry will be our nephew."

Maryanne was pleased that Henry and Miss King had found happiness with each other. Perhaps it would not be long before her own wedding to Richard, and Emily's to George.

When they were ready to depart, Lady Malden wished them a pleasant day.

"I must return another time, as it is quite tiring with so many wonders to admire. Be sure to rest now and then."

Maryanne wondered if the lady was more tired than she cared to admit and perhaps wished she might join them after all. But she was reassured when Lady Malden said she was expecting a visit from her friend, Lady Grey.

"Go and enjoy yourselves," she told them. "You shall tell me all about it when you return."

When they arrived at Sydenham, it was already busy with people and noise as they made their way to the entrance of the Crystal Palace. Once inside, Maryanne was astonished at the high glass arched ceiling and noticed the huge organ Richard had mentioned.

She could see at once that it might be difficult to keep together, especially if they each had different interests.

"Why don't we arrange to meet for luncheon at one o'clock?" Richard suggested. "In case we happen to lose each other."

"Splendid idea," George agreed. "Emily and I shall wander about to see what captures our interest."

"And you must join us, Charlotte," Emily added at once. "I suspect Maryanne and Richard will wish to visit the most boring sections."

This was delivered with a smile and Maryanne had no doubt Emily was ensuring she and Richard had time on their own. She would return the kindness later in the day.

Charlotte seemed preoccupied, glancing about as she had at the theatre. Maryanne felt a pang of unease and a suspicion the girl was planning more mischief. She was reassured when Charlotte agreed to accompany her sister and George. Hopefully, they would not neglect her.

They parted at the concert venue, once ascertaining it would be after lunch before the first concert. They all agreed it would be a good way to end their visit.

One of the first exhibitions Maryanne and Richard viewed was the variety of fine art courts, such as the Egyptian and Renaissance areas. They were in awe of the fountains, the full-size prehistoric animals and the architectural wonders of the building itself.

Finally noticing it was time for luncheon, Maryanne and Richard soon found Emily and George already waiting for them. Maryanne knew from Emily's agitation that something was amiss.

"Oh, Maryanne, we turned away for the merest second and suddenly, Charlotte was no longer there!"

What a trouble the girl was proving, much as Maryanne had feared.

"Please find a seat for Emily and yourself, George. Richard and I shall find Charlotte."

Persuading Emily that they did not want to lose anyone else, Maryanne and Richard set off to search for the missing girl. Much easier said than done they soon discovered, as they tried to find their way through the bustling mass of people, many of the women in their best crinolines. Maryanne's own skirts swayed more than once as she squeezed past several groups milling around the exhibits.

"I have a suspicion we should make our way to the meeting rooms," Maryanne suggested.

"I suspect you're right," Richard agreed. "I noticed Charlotte's interest in them earlier."

Maryanne smiled as she took his arm. His understanding and observation skills was one of the reasons she had fallen in love with this man. Besides which, they were most often in one accord, so far at least.

Finally, they discovered where today's meetings were taking place. As soon as Maryanne saw the title of the lecture, Mesmerism, she was certain they would find Charlotte inside.

At first, Maryanne observed that the audience mainly consisted of men, with a few females perhaps accompanying a husband.

Then her full attention focused on the man about to address the audience from a small stage. If she were not mistaken, it was the gentleman who had been speaking with Charlotte and Mr Taylor at the soirée.

She was about to whisper to Richard when she noticed Charlotte sitting at one side. But she was not alone. Had she perhaps merely sat down beside someone? Then she noticed Charlotte turn to the man with a smile as he whispered to her.

Maryanne drew Richard's attention to them. "Let's sit here at the back to observe, please," she murmured. She wanted to see what was taking place.

Her thoughts were in turmoil again as she tried to make sense of her cousin being in the company of an unknown man. She could not see enough of him to be certain, but did not think it was Mr Taylor.

How had Charlotte managed to meet with someone again? Unless it was the man from the theatre. Could this be the person with whom she had been corresponding? At least she should soon find out the identity of the man on the stage, if not for the reason he had been at Lady Eldritch's soiree.

Chapter Twelve

Forcing herself to wait until the meeting was over before confronting Charlotte, Maryanne found her interest caught as the talk progressed.

Mesmerism. She knew too well what that could mean for some. But how could Charlotte be interested in a practice that had caused her so much horror and distress at Mulberry Manor?

She tried to obtain better view of the man beside Charlotte but was too far away. Yet his obvious height and a vague memory suggested she had seen him before. A terrible idea came to mind but she dismissed it as being too fanciful. Still… the fact that this meeting was about mesmerism suggested it might not be completely unlikely.

The gentleman on the stage, who had been introduced as a Doctor Beckwith, was explaining an experiment that had allowed surgery without pain due to the patient being mesmerised. Although small of stature, his even toned, commanding voice soon had the audience in his enthral.

"It is possible to alter the state of a patient's mind so that he or she will feel no pain, and mesmerism can also be used for other ailments of the human body and mind. You may find this difficult to comprehend, but I have heard that one might even perform an amputation of the limb, causing the patient no distress, if he or she has been mesmerised first."

Maryanne was not the only one present to gasp at that idea. She gave the doctor her full attention, hoping Richard understood her need to hear more. She was fascinated despite her distaste and had no doubt at all that some of what he said was possible.

"Some of you may have heard of the renowned Doctor Elliotson," Doctor Beckwith continued. "He practised mesmerism with great success, yet some wished to discredit him, refusing to accept the scientific proof he offered. Even after he had alleviated pain, helped with sleep and illness problems and cured disease, he had to implore the medical profession to dispassionately examine this subject. I have certainly done so and have proved its worth, as I shall continue to do."

Maryanne glanced at Charlotte to find her attention completely focused on the stage. The girl was such a puzzle and yet she had never been quite herself since the events at the manor. Did she perhaps hope to consult this doctor?

Suddenly, she stared in disbelief. Charlotte was being led to the stage by the man beside her! Starting up from her seat, she felt Richard's hand on her arm.

"Wait, Maryanne. We cannot interfere and Charlotte is not even aware we are here."

Maryanne knew he spoke good sense. Better to observe and see what might entail. But what if they had not discovered Charlotte here and had known nothing of this?

Biting her lip as her cousin stood on the stage, Maryanne could not believe Charlotte had agreed to this public display. Was she already under another person's influence? The man who had led her to the front, perhaps?

Craning to try and see exactly what was about to happen, Richard's hand covering hers, Maryanne could scarcely contain herself, yet curiosity had taken over from fear.

Charlotte seemed unconcerned at standing on a platform in full view of the audience and made such a pretty picture in her rose-pink gown and straw bonnet, tendrils of her light brown hair around her neck.

It was difficult to see Charlotte's eyes from her seat, but Maryanne became convinced her cousin was already being influenced by the doctor who was now speaking to her in a low voice. Then he turned to the audience.

"This young lady is an interesting case. She suspects she already succumbed to mesmerism in the past. Is that not true, my dear?"

"Yes." Charlotte stared ahead as she replied.

Maryanne gripped Richard's hand. It was a terrible memory for all of them, but how much more for Charlotte.

"Her memories are disturbed, however, and she seeks a cure. Is that not so?" he addressed Charlotte who nodded.

"It is."

"Now I want you to relax as much as possible and keep your attention focused on me. I am merely going to show these good people how effective this treatment can be."

Charlotte stared at the doctor who had turned sideways to the audience.

Maryanne longed to stop these proceedings and take her cousin safely away from the gaze of so many.

Richard's pressure on her hand told her he knew too well what she was thinking.

"Wait a little longer, Maryanne," he said.

Biting her lip again, Maryanne watched, interested against her will. She knew this practise had become popular, with literary figures such as the Trollopes and Elizabeth Barret Browning fascinated with both mesmerism and spiritualism. Even the writer Charles Dickens had performed mesmerism on his wife and others, seemingly to great success.

Not that it reassured her.

Keeping her attention on Charlotte, Maryanne saw the doctor reach out a hand and speak quietly to her cousin and next minute, she gasped when Charlotte's head sagged lifelessly.

The doctor supported her at once and another man appeared with a chair for her. They sat Charlotte gently down and Maryanne watched fearfully as the girl straightened again to focus on the doctor.

Maryanne strained to hear the words he spoke but they were seated too far back, and perhaps they were meant only for Charlotte's ears. She stared intently at the stage hoping this terrible escapade would not make her cousin even worse. Horrified, she saw the doctor take a pin in his hand.

"Watch how the young lady now feels no pain."

And he pressed the pin into the hand Charlotte held out. Maryanne gripped Richard's arm to stop herself from calling out. But from Charlotte there was not the slightest reaction of pain or surprise.

A few seconds later, after some more words from the doctor, Charlotte stood and faced the audience.

Her clear voice rang out. "Thank you, Doctor

Beckwith." She gave a small half curtsey to the audience who immediately clapped.

Maryanne put a hand to her mouth, horrified that Charlotte had subjected herself to such an experiment under public scrutiny. The people watching were acting as though they had enjoyed a spectacle. Which she supposed they had in a way, albeit with her poor cousin as the main attraction.

As soon as the audience began to disperse, Maryanne and Richard walked towards the front of the room, anxious to rescue Charlotte. But as they neared, Maryanne saw her cousin being led away through another door by the man who had sat beside her.

This time, Maryanne didn't wait for Richard's advice and she rushed after them. But the door was now locked and there was no sign of the doctor, or her cousin and mysterious companion.

"Where have they gone?" Maryanne turned to Richard in distress. "We cannot leave her to those men, Richard." She shrugged off his attempt to take her arm. "We must search for her. There *must* be another way out from that room."

Before Richard could react, Maryanne hurried to the entrance of the meeting room, now empty of the departing audience.

Puzzling what to do, she noticed what seemed to be an official standing to one side.

"Please, sir, may we bother you for a moment? I need to know if there is another exit to that meeting room, for my cousin seems to have disappeared."

Looking down at her from his great height, the man stared at her then Richard and addressed himself to Richard.

"What seems to be the problem, sir?"

Maryanne wanted to scream at the condescension towards her but the priority was to find Charlotte.

Richard glanced at Maryanne before replying, his eyes understanding her annoyance.

"This lady's cousin was taking part in an experiment on the stage inside that meeting room. At the end, she was led to another room which was locked behind her. We need to find her at once."

Puffing out his chest at Richard's authoritative tone, the official wasted no more time.

"Follow me please. No doubt the young lady is being looked after."

But by whom? Maryanne knew there was no point in voicing her fear and hurried beside Richard and the official. How could they return to the others without Charlotte, knowing she was in the hands of two gentlemen?

At least the official knew where to look and soon they were approaching a small door. As soon as he turned the handle, the door swung open. The room was empty.

"Is this the correct room?" Maryanne asked. "Leading to the larger meeting room?"

"Look, there's the other door," Richard said, hurrying over to it.

Maryanne watched in disbelief when that door also opened right away. All three of them glanced inside to find it empty.

"But where has she gone?" Maryanne cried.

"I'm sorry, Miss, but as you see there's no one here. P'rhaps she's waiting for you somewhere else."

"Thank you for your assistance," Richard said,

taking Maryanne's arm.

Once the official had gone back to his post, Maryanne turned on Richard.

"I cannot believe this! Where is Charlotte? And with whom?"

More importantly, what had the doctor done to her mind?

Chapter Thirteen

Trying to remain calm, and thankful for Richard's presence, Maryanne hurried back towards Emily and George, with no idea what to tell them about Charlotte. Although pleased she had seen so many wonderful sights already, some of her delight in the day had dissipated.

As they approached the eating area, Maryanne noticed Emily and George first, evidently in conversation with someone. It was only when George moved aside that Maryanne saw the person.

"Look, Richard!" She made him pause.

"Charlotte? She must have come straight here while we were searching for her." He frowned.

"Let's not mention seeing her at the meeting. I should like to observe her for now." Maryanne was astonished that the girl appeared quite as usual.

There was no sign of the gentleman who had sat beside her, however, and Maryanne was frustrated once again that she had failed to identify him.

Maryanne approached the small group. "I'm happy to see you are here, Charlotte," she said.

"Charlotte has been telling us of a most interesting meeting," Emily said.

Maryanne glanced at Richard who raised an eyebrow. Perhaps they were about to find out more.

"Ah, so that's where you've been. We thought you lost. Do tell us about it, Charlotte," Maryanne said.

Charlotte turned guileless eyes on Maryanne. "It was a fascinating talk by a prominent doctor about helping people without medication. Is that not wonderful?"

Maryanne glanced at Richard, frowning at her cousin's enthusiasm. What about Charlotte's own part in it?

"And you were listening the whole time?" Richard asked.

"Why, of course, until the end."

Maryanne was perplexed. Did Charlotte have no recollection of standing on the stage in front of so many people?

"Did anything interesting happen while you were there?" she asked.

Charlotte looked confused before replying. "I don't understand what you mean. The doctor's talk was most interesting."

Maryanne frowned. It would seem Charlotte indeed had no memory of her part in the meeting.

"Surely you did not attend by yourself?" Maryanne had to ask. "Did you perhaps meet Mr Taylor?"

This time, Charlotte turned away as she replied. "Why are you asking so many questions, cousin? Where did *you* go?"

Maryanne was taken aback at the sudden coldness in Charlotte's voice and manner and wasn't sure how to respond.

"We're merely concerned that you didn't feel neglected while we all enjoyed our own entertainment," Richard said.

Maryanne smiled at him, thankful he had found the right response. Charlotte merely nodded and addressed

Emily and George.

"Shall we have luncheon now," she asked, taking Emily's arm.

The moment passed as they found a vacant table to enjoy their light repast, although Maryanne continued to be perplexed. Charlotte showed no signs of distress or vagueness, but she also had not once mentioned the word mesmerism in relation to the talk. Nor had she admitted to meeting the doctor before.

After they had eaten and rested enough, Charlotte pleaded a headache. Although Maryanne had energy enough to look at other attractions, they all decided to go home to Lady Malden's together.

"I promise we shall return to this and other attractions one day by ourselves, Maryanne," Richard whispered to her as they secured their carriage.

"I look forward to it." Especially if only by themselves.

When they returned home, Lady Malden had a surprise for them before Richard and George departed.

"Emily, Charlotte, your brother Henry called here earlier and has arranged to meet us at the park tomorrow. He suggested the venue as he will not be alone."

"Oh, that's wonderful," Emily said. "Miss King must be accompanying him, with her little boy, I assume."

"Evidently, that is true, "Lady Malden confirmed. "Henry was most anxious to see you all again."

Maryanne was pleased they would meet in better circumstances than last Christmas and she was as eager to see the little boy as Emily. Although Charlotte smiled, she said not a word and excused herself as soon as possible.

Maryanne managed a few words with Richard before he left, longing to discuss the puzzle of Charlotte. Fortunately, Emily and George were content to remain talking to Lady Malden of all they had seen at the Crystal Palace while Maryanne and Richard took a short walk in the rear garden.

"Do you think Charlotte is quite well, Richard? She seems a little distant – even more so than usual." Maryanne took his proffered arm.

"I don't understand exactly what happened but I agree there is a strangeness about her behaviour. I confess it's beyond me to offer either a reason or a solution."

Maryanne could only agree. "It all began with mesmerism; perhaps this latest episode has made her worse rather than helping her, if that was the purpose. I should very much like to speak to her companion whoever he is."

"You could try confronting Charlotte again, on your own. Perhaps even admit you saw her at the meeting?"

Maryanne struggled with that idea, afraid to make matters worse. Yet, something was amiss with her cousin and Maryanne longed to help if she could.

Chapter Fourteen

Everyone was in high spirits the following fine autumn day as they dressed in outdoor gowns, lacing boots and light shawls suitable for a walk in the park. Maryanne was looking forward to seeing Henry again but couldn't deny her eagerness to spend more time with Richard before they parted.

Lady Malden outshone them as always, her new parasol ready to avert the risk of the dreaded sunspots. Maryanne had no such dread and lifted her face to welcome any fleeting warmth before the onset of winter.

The paths and walkways were already busy when their little party met Richard and George, both handsomely turned out as usual. Maryanne gladly took Richard's arm as they strolled along behind the others. She was pleased to see that Charlotte was more animated today and relieved they could all enjoy a leisurely walk together.

They were admiring two splendid horses and riders when a voice hailed them.

"Hello! Look who's here." Henry grinned as he and his companions approached.

"Henry!" Emily ran into her brother's embrace, then impulsively hugged the pretty lady beside him. "And Miss King!"

Maryanne noticed the fair-haired small child watching from his perambulator, a thumb stuck in his mouth. While Henry greeted his sisters and Lady Malden, Maryanne crouched down beside the boy.

"Hello, little Harry. You've grown since last I saw you."

After a few moments while he stared at her face, the boy's mouth curved into a wide smile and he reached out to grasp her hair, gurgling happily.

"You seem a very smart little boy and it's as well my hair is pinned out of reach, I think." Maryanne laughed as she continued speaking to the contented child.

"I see you're a natural with children, cousin," Henry said, waiting until Maryanne had stood up before embracing her. "It's good to see you again. You must come and be reacquainted with Felicity."

Maryanne smiled to see Richard take her place beside the boy and she had a sudden image of him as a father with his own child. Quickly pushing such a delicious thought aside, Maryanne greeted Felicity King with pleasure.

"I'm delighted to see you again, Miss Robertson," Felicity said.

"Please use my given name, for I suspect we shall be cousins one day. I'm so pleased we're all together again. You are well?"

"Very well, thank you, Maryanne. I have much to be grateful for. As you see, my little Harry is thriving which is in no small measure due to Henry."

Maryanne noticed the loving glance that passed between the couple and had no doubt they planned a future together.

"Your son is delightful and I wish you all much happiness."

Felicity unexpectedly embraced her and Maryanne hoped they might see each other again.

While they were in conversation with each other, a smart older nanny was walking from the opposite direction pushing a baby in a perambulator, a small boy beside her carrying a hoop. They stopped nearby to allow the little boy to play and soon his happy cries caught the attention of the men.

Maryanne wasn't quite certain what happened next but the hoop seemed to run away from the boy and all at once, Richard, George and Henry set of in pursuit to the delight of the boy who now had playmates.

The ladies strolled along laughing at their antics as the hoop was caught but soon rolling on its way again, with Henry running alongside the boy. Maryanne could see how good a father he would prove to little Harry.

It was only as they turned a corner, that Maryanne realised one of their party was missing. Felicity was still beside her, while Emily and Lady Malden conversed. But where was Charlotte?

Annoyance mingled with her concern, as Maryanne glanced around their immediate area, hoping the girl had merely rested at a bench. Unwilling to spoil the men's fun with the little boy, she quietly spoke to Felicity.

"Please excuse me, Felicity, but Charlotte seems to have disappeared and I'm a little concerned as she complained of a headache last night."

"Oh, of course. But we can alert everyone to look for her."

"No, please don't alarm anyone. If you join Emily and Lady Malden, who will be happy to fuss over little

Harry, I shall go and find Charlotte. Perhaps she is merely looking at the plants and flowers, an excuse you might use if anyone remarks on our absence."

Obviously unhappy that she alone was aware of this, Felicity nodded. "I shall do my best but please take care and return as quickly as possible."

Ensuring no one else noticed, Maryanne hurried back through the park, looking this way and that, hoping Charlotte had indeed stopped to rest or admire a floral display. Not that she quite believed her own story.

Careful not to attract attention, Maryanne slowed to a brisk walk, aware she was an unaccompanied young lady. As was Charlotte.

When she reached a tree-filled area, Maryanne glanced to her right and paused. A flash of reflected sunlight caught her attention and she was shocked to see a man and woman half hidden by an oak tree. Surely not Charlotte? She could not be *this* foolish, could she?

Strolling round to one side of the path, Maryanne tried for a clearer view. The couple were not in an embrace as she had feared, but were in earnest conversation. She caught a peek of a lace-trimmed bonnet and her resolve hardened. It was indeed Charlotte, in company with what appeared to be the same man from the meeting.

Maryanne straightened her shoulders and prepared to confront them, when there was a touch on her shoulder.

"There you are, Maryanne. I was worried where you had gone, though suspected it was to do with your cousin, again. I noticed she was missing."

Although pleased to see Richard, Maryanne was determined to identify the man with Charlotte.

"Quick," she whispered. "We must rescue Charlotte."

"I doubt she is requiring, or would welcome, our assistance, my dear."

Maryanne gasped as she saw Charlotte lean into the man's embrace, willingly it appeared. The man seemed tender enough, but this was completely untoward and foolish of her cousin to be in such a compromising situation. She obviously required rescuing from herself.

"This is unacceptable, Richard. I must speak to her." It mattered not if he was in agreement, for he would not stop her this time.

Just then, Charlotte looked their way and immediately removed herself from the man's arms as she whispered to him.

By the time Maryanne approached Charlotte, she was alone.

"Maryanne! Why are you following me?"

Keeping her frustration in check, Maryanne took her cousin's arm. "We were concerned when we realised you were missing. Come, the others will have noticed our absence."

"But I am quite all right." Charlotte went with them meekly enough, after one quick glance behind.

Maryanne glanced at Richard, her eyebrows raised in question. What should she say? Yet she had seen enough to make her more direct this time.

"Charlotte, who is the man you have been meeting?"

Charlotte stopped walking and turned, her blue

eyes sparkling. "He is a friend who is helping me to make sense of this past year."

Not at all reassured by such a reply, Maryanne frowned. "But who is he? How do you know him and what is his name?"

"You ask too many questions, cousin. You are making my head ache again."

Maryanne stood in dismay as Charlotte strode on ahead, refusing to heed anything else Maryanne might say.

"This is not normal," she said to Richard. "Does she not know his name?"

"I assume she is not ready to share her secrets, or is unable to do so perhaps."

"Then we must find this man." Maryanne was even more determined she would confront him should he appear again. Quite how this was to be accomplished she knew not, but she would find a way.

Another thought struck her. How did Charlotte and the man contrive to meet so easily? Did he keep watch on the house so that he might follow them?

Chapter Fifteen

Maryanne was aware of so little time being left in London and was determined to enjoy it. The ladies had one more outing, to Hatchard's bookshop at Piccadilly before resting for a final evening ball. A visit that pleased Maryanne more than any other type of shop.

She was amazed again at the bustling streets as they strolled along, sweeping their long skirts away from the dirt and detritus whenever possible. Cries of 'buy my lavender' and 'nice ripe cherries, my lovely' followed them along.

More than one urchin child darted precariously between carts and horses, some trying to earn a penny by sweeping a clean path for a well-turned-out gentleman or such like. Maryanne was horrified at the number of girls amongst the boys, matted hair tumbling around grimy faces. She couldn't bear to think about their little lives surrounded by thieves and pickpockets, and no doubt houses of ill-repute.

Yet what could she do for them? Offering a penny would bring a hoard of children upon them clambering for more and it would make no difference to their lives. It did, however, make her consider the little she could do in her own parish to ensure poorer children were fed and educated where possible. Her father and mother already did so much but their resources were limited.

Perhaps when she and Richard were married, she might find more worthwhile work to do, if he were agreeable of course, and if she did not become a mother too soon. But that was in the future, delightful though her daydream might be, as they had not even discussed where they would make their home.

Maryanne's musings ended when they reached Hatchard's with its moss green doors and curved leaded windows. Once inside, she stared in delight at the array of books and wooden staircases promising more exploration.

Mindful that no one else might be as interested in books, she chose a small poetry pamphlet that might suit her Papa, and a small book on the constellations for herself that she could later share with Richard.

When Maryanne reluctantly followed the others to the door, Lady Malden took charge again.

"Now we must have some tea and cakes, since this is your final outing in town, my dears," Lady Malden suggested, although none would have the temerity to argue otherwise.

Marching ahead, she brushed aside a little urchin who had approached too close. Not unkindly, but with the certainty of her class that he had nothing to do with her.

But Maryanne soon discovered it was not the great lady he was approaching. She happened to see him speedily pass a note to Charlotte before he scurried into the crowd. Feigning interest in a shop window, Charlotte paused a moment and glanced at the note before pushing it into her pocket.

Maryanne frowned. How she would like to see what was written! She must content herself with keeping watch on her cousin instead.

They had no sooner entered the tea house when

they found Mr Taylor already there. Maryanne was astonished to recognise his companion as Doctor Beckwith. She wondered again how well they knew each other. Surely this was but a coincidence they happened to be here?

Mr Taylor immediately stood to greet them but did not bother to introduce his friend who was now perusing a notebook. Charlotte, however, paused as she stared at the seated man before accepting Mr Taylor's compliments.

"I hope you might keep me a dance at the ball this evening, Miss Harrington," he said.

"All my nieces will be pleased to fill their dance cards, Mr Taylor, and it is hoped there will be space for you on each one." Lady Malden swept onwards to their table, gathering her flock of girls behind her.

Maryanne noticed the quick inclination of his head as the doctor eventually returned Charlotte's glance at him and she hoped he would not be at the ball. But his association with Mr Taylor filled her with unease and she longed to discuss it with Richard.

Thankfully, the welcome tea in delicate China cups revived them and each chose a small cake to sustain them for the remainder of the morning. But Maryanne's pleasure was once again tempered by the knowledge that Charlotte was keeping too many secrets from them.

Lady Malden's house was in pleasant chaos as each of the ladies primped and powdered in readiness for the ball that evening, the poor maids hurrying about with ewers of hot water and a readiness to aid with hair styles and gown fasteners.

Maryanne suffered the tightening of her corset to enhance her shape, albeit at the cost of some comfort, before stepping into the wide hoop that would hold her skirts from her lower limbs. When the silky pale green crinoline was in place, she smiled at her reflection, her shining hair in a more elaborate style than she was used to; the bulk caught up on top of her head with a few wavy curls hanging down on either side of her face.

"Thank you, Simmons," she told the maid. "You have a clever touch with hair."

Simmons smiled. "It's a pleasure when the hair is so thick as yours, Miss."

Emily and Charlotte both shone in their finery, the first in a light cerulean blue and Charlotte in a deep rose pink. Lady Malden was magnificent as always, resplendent in a deep cobalt blue gown, hair enclosed in a jewelled turban more reminiscent of previous decades.

Although not far out of town, their carriage made slow progress, darkness descending when they left Lady Malden's house. As they neared the lavish abode of her friend, Lady Grey, several carriages had already drawn up or were in the process of departing, the occupants discharged.

Large torch flares lit their path to the front entrance where liveried footmen bade them welcome. Maryanne shared Emily's pleasure since she rarely had the opportunity to attend so fine an event, especially with Richard. It was at her first ball at Mulberry Manor when she had fallen in love with him. She even wore the same ball gown, although without a mask this time.

The large house was awash with hordes of ladies and gentlemen in their finery, the wide crinolines in various bright colours, apart from duller shades on some of the older matrons.

Maryanne, Charlotte and Emily were greeted by their host and hostess, both of whom welcomed them with pleasure.

"Thank you for providing such a lavish event for my young ladies," Lady Malden said to her friend.

"Tosh, my dear," Lady Grey said. "We never need an excuse for a ball and London has been so dull." She smiled at each of them in turn. "Now be sure to fill your dance cards and enjoy every minute of being young and beautiful," she told them.

Maryanne reflected that the good lady might not have been so welcoming had she daughters of her own to marry off, then immediately admonished herself for such an uncharitable thought. When she saw the gathered throng, she suspected any gentleman present might have his pick from the vast number of females.

The first dance had not yet been announced when Mr Taylor appeared beside Charlotte and insisted on at least one dance. Hoping he would not turn his attention to her next, Maryanne was pleased to see that Richard and George had arrived.

"Please excuse us a moment," she said. Maryanne took Emily's arm and they went to greet the two gentlemen they most wished to see.

"I confess I'm relieved we did not need to write Mr Taylor's name in our card," Emily whispered. "Is that very bad of me?"

Maryanne squeezed her cousin's hand as she laughed. "My feelings exactly, Emily. And you could never be bad."

However, Maryanne shared her cousin's reluctance

and wondered about Charlotte's true feelings towards Mr Taylor, as he was not the tall companion they had seen her with before.

Her musings were pleasantly diverted when Richard took her arm, leaving Emily and George to their own greetings.

"May I compliment you on your beauty this evening, Maryanne, although it's merely enhanced by your finery."

A warm glow suffused her at the look in his eyes, more than the fulsome words, and she unfurled her fan to cool her face.

"Then we are well matched," she replied, "for not one man can rival you this evening, or any other."

His tall frame suited the formal trousers and dress jacket and she marvelled again that they had found each other, long after those childhood years when she had been allowed in the schoolroom at his country home.

"The first and last dance must be mine, please, my love," Richard said. "And any others you might spare between, especially if it's a waltz."

Maryanne willingly added his name to her card. "I've written you against the dance directly before supper for I could not bear to take it with anyone else."

"Excellent. And I'll endeavour to get through a few dances with some of the young ladies who might otherwise become wallflowers."

Satisfied in their love for each other, Maryanne allowed Richard to lead her to the dance floor for the first polka. Among the couples, she noticed Charlotte take her place with Mr Taylor. Emily stood up with George and even Lady Malden was partnered by a large military looking gentleman.

As the orchestra struck up the first notes and the music swept Maryanne through the lively steps, she wished she might not have to part from Richard so soon. At least they could enjoy this evening together.

Although she lost sight of her cousins while dancing with various young hopefuls, she looked forward to meeting them at the supper provided. Delighted that the next dance was a waltz, Maryanne gladly took her place before Richard and gave no more thought to anyone else. As always, the music transported her around the room, her feet light as she and Richard danced together as though alone.

"I would never wish to dance a waltz with anyone but you," she whispered as the music ended.

"My sentiments exactly." Richard offered his arm as supper was announced. "I think it's a clear sky this evening. Why don't we take some air after the refreshments and discover what constellations might be visible?"

"That would be perfect. But first I must have some lemonade or I shall not be able to speak."

They passed Emily and George on their way to the light supper but Maryanne could not see Charlotte or Mr Taylor. Perhaps there were too many people in the way. Trying to ignore the tiny knot of disquiet beginning in her abdomen, Maryanne managed to eat a few of the delicious bites once she had quenched her thirst.

"Shall we slip outside?" Richard soon asked.

Maryanne needed no second thought, glad to escape into the cool night air away from the heat from the myriad candles and mingling scents of people and food. The extensive grounds allowed for various types of garden areas and they stepped through the open balcony door and down the steps to the lantern-lit lawn.

Pausing by a stone statue of a Roman goddess, Richard put his arm around Maryanne's shoulder. "Look how clear the sky is tonight. I wish we could catch sight of the famous comet but must make do with what we *can* see."

Enjoying the warmth of his arm, Maryanne snuggled closer as she looked up at the thousands of stars. "I confess their pattern is beyond my recognition but it's so vast and beautiful. How insignificant we are, don't you think?"

"Except to each other, of course." Richard looked down into her eyes and she turned into his arms.

His lips claimed hers and she melted against his chest, experiencing a complete sense of belonging as she returned his kiss.

"Ah, Maryanne." Richard raised his head to look at her again. "We must be together in every sense very soon for I dislike being parted from you."

Maryanne gave herself up to another, deeper kiss and wished it need never stop.

"I shall call upon your father soon, I promise," Richard said at last. "Then we can begin making our arrangements."

"He'll be delighted to see you, as will Mama."

Maryanne still had no knowledge of where they might live nor how soon their marriage might take place, but she was secure in his love and promises and that was enough for now.

They had scarcely strolled any length on their return to the house when Maryanne became aware of voices nearby, one of them female.

She touched Richard's arm to hold him back. "Listen, does that not sound like Charlotte?"

The sound came from beyond the small orchard and they walked towards it as though merely taking the air.

Two male voices, and one female sounding increasingly like Charlotte, disturbed the night air. It was the note of panic in the female voice that persuaded Maryanne they must investigate. She whispered her intention to Richard.

Nodding, he took her hand as they crept towards the sound.

"I do not wish to go with you!"

Charlotte's clear voice rang out as Maryanne and Richard inched closer until they could see to whom the other voices belonged.

"That's Doctor Beckwith," Maryanne exclaimed. "And Mr Taylor. Are they trying to abduct Charlotte?"

Beyond caring about being seen and concerned only for her cousin, Maryanne walked boldly forward.

"Oh, there you are, Charlotte. We feared we had lost you. Good evening again, Mr Taylor."

Three pairs of eyes regarded Maryanne and she was thankful to feel Richard's hand on her shoulder from behind. Hoping her cousin would not cause more problems, Maryanne approached Charlotte.

"Are you ready to return to the ballroom, cousin dear? Your sister was looking for you."

With a quick glance at the two men, Charlotte lowered her head. "I should like that, thank you."

"Do you return too, Mr Taylor?" Richard asked.

Maryanne had not missed the fact that the doctor

had edged further away from them during this exchange.

"Not at the moment. I must say goodbye to my friend first."

Charlotte allowed Maryanne to take her arm as they returned to the house, but she said not another word. And although it was dark in the gardens apart from the lanterns, Maryanne had not mistaken the look of venom that the doctor sent her way when they came upon her cousin.

She very much feared she had made an enemy and for once, she was happy to know they would soon be safely on their way from London and returning north to Mulberry Manor, before she continued to her own home in Scotland.

But what had the doctor intended with Charlotte and what was Mr Taylor's part in it? Should he be trusted or not?

Chapter Sixteen

The dancing had resumed after the refreshments when Maryanne and Richard returned to the ballroom with Charlotte. The girl had still not explained what took place outside but went straight to sit beside Lady Malden after the merest 'thank you'.

"This is beyond a slight concern now," Maryanne said to Richard. "I do not trust that doctor, nor Mr Taylor for that matter."

"Perhaps we should confront Taylor when he returns," Richard suggested.

But although Maryanne kept watch for him between dances, there was no further sign of Mr Taylor. Charlotte sat meekly beside Lady Malden who was in animated conversation with the lady next to her.

It was nearing the end of the evening and Maryanne was enjoying what might be her last dance with Richard, when she happened to glance across the room. Charlotte was no longer in her seat.

Maryanne faltered as she looked around the dancers. No sign of her cousin. Emily and George danced past so she was not with them. Even Lady Malden had stood up with the military gentleman again. Offering Charlotte the opportunity to go where she wished.

"Charlotte is nowhere in sight," Maryanne told Richard when they next came together.

"Perhaps she is resting upstairs?" he suggested.

"Or perhaps she has gone outside again." Maryanne was more convinced of this by the knot in her abdomen that warned her Charlotte was not inside the house.

"We must go and check, Richard. I'm sorry, but anything might have happened to her."

"I agree, Maryanne. Let's not linger." He took her arm.

Thankful again for his constant understanding, Maryanne strolled with him towards the open doors. Let anyone who noticed them assume they were seizing one last opportunity to take a walk together before the ball ended.

As soon as they were outside, they hurried to the gardens but could see no sign of Charlotte. They had reached the furthest edge, near the road, when Maryanne heard raised voices again. Male only this time.

Not stopping to consider any danger, she broke free from Richard and rushed forward, desperate to seek the source and hopefully find her cousin.

She stopped suddenly at the sight before her. A figure lay on the road, Mr Taylor standing over him. But where was Charlotte?

"What on earth! What have you done, Mr Taylor?"

Then Maryanne heard the faintest sound of a horse's snicker and looked to the road.

"Richard! I think there's a carriage beyond that tree."

But before Maryanne and Richard could move towards it, Mr Taylor had darted between the trees and next minute they watched helplessly as a carriage and four rattled off along the road as though pursued.

Maryanne grasped Richard. "I'm certain Charlotte is in that carriage. Oh, Richard, what are we to do now? How could Mr Taylor betray us so?"

A groan from the ground reminded them of the man lying injured, and Maryanne knelt down to ascertain how badly he was hurting.

Perhaps he could enlighten them as to what had happened, once able to speak. Maryanne noticed his long frame and suspected he was the companion they had previously seen with Charlotte. Hopefully, they would find out more about him at last.

She was about to make way for Richard to help the man up when she stood up suddenly in disbelief.

"You! How can this be? Where is my cousin?"

Thankful he was able to stand with Richard's help, although holding a hand to his bruised head, Maryanne was staring at a man she had thought never to see or hear of again.

"Miss Robertson? Mr Carmichael. I tried to stop them abducting your cousin but was overpowered."

"Stop who? Mr Taylor, obviously, but who else?" Although she had a very good idea who might be involved.

"A doctor of the mind, although he does not deserve his title."

"But what does he want with Charlotte, and why is Mr Taylor involved? For that matter, why are you here?" Maryanne was so perplexed that she hoped some answers would soon be forthcoming.

"Please give me a moment to compose myself and I shall explain, as far as I am able."

"I certainly hope that is possible, Mr Mathieson."

Maryanne could scarcely believe that this man,

whom she had last seen in distressing circumstances at Mulberry Manor the previous year, was now standing before her. And that he had been spending time with Charlotte. It was beyond her comprehension.

"I think it best if we return to the ball." Richard's practical voice intervened. "We must alert Lady Malden and Emily then decide what to do for the carriage will be long gone by now."

"But Charlotte? I cannot bear to think of her with that man."

Mr Mathieson coughed, as they turned towards the house. "If it helps at all, Miss Robertson, I believe Mr Taylor will not allow any real harm to come to your cousin."

Not at all reassured by his words, considering she was in the hands of that sinister doctor, Maryanne did not speak, wishing only to hear what this man knew.

When they stepped back inside the balcony doors, the final dance had just ended. Edging their way discreetly around the room, they found several seats outside the ballroom in a quiet corridor.

"Will you stay with Mr Mathieson please, Richard, while I seek out Emily, George and Lady Malden?"

"Of course. But make haste before the guests begin leaving."

Her urgency conveying itself to the others at once, it was only a matter of minutes before Maryanne returned with them.

Offering Lady Malden his seat, Richard stood keeping watch over Mr Mathieson, who seemed resigned to the inquisition about to commence.

Emily reacted first, taking a step back from the silent man, her eyes wide with disbelief.

"No! It cannot be Mr Mathieson." She looked around in fear. "But where is my sister? What have you done with Charlotte?"

Maryanne touched the girl's arm. "Let him speak, Emily."

But Lady Malden took charge.

"This is not the place to have a private conversation. We shall make our farewells to the hosts and this gentleman shall come home with us."

"But Charlotte?" Emily cried.

"We shall find your sister, I promise," Richard said. He frowned at Mr Mathieson. "Once we discover what is going on."

The carriage soon conveyed them to Lady Malden's where Mr Mathieson once more became the centre of their attention as he began his explanation.

"Miss Harrington and I have been corresponding for several months…"

"I knew it!" Emily interrupted. "At least I had no knowledge that you were the person with whom my sister corresponded."

Mr Mathieson glanced at Emily. "I mean your sister no harm. In fact, I care very much for her."

Emily gasped but said no more.

"Miss Harrington has been under considerable stress since the terrible incident involving my sister at Mulberry Manor."

He paused and Maryanne could see how affected he was at the memory.

"Charlotte knew of my connection with those who agreed that mesmerism can bring great results." He glanced again at Emily as she moaned, her hand to her mouth. "As well as cause harm in certain circumstances."

This time, he looked at his clasped hands as he seemed to choose his words.

"Please go on, Mr Mathieson, "Maryanne urged, "for we are wasting time. My cousin has been abducted and must be rescued."

"Of course, you are quite correct, and I only wish I'd prevented it."

Richard stirred beside Maryanne. "Then be quick, Mathieson."

The man nodded." Suffice to say, we were pleased to meet again when you came to London. But we couldn't know that events would overtake us when Mr Taylor introduced Charlotte to Doctor Beckwith."

"Does the doctor wish her harm?" Lady Malden asked.

Mr Mathieson started as though he'd forgotten her presence.

"I don't know. I think it's more a question of experimentation, which is still under scrutiny. You may recall stories of a Doctor Elliotson and how other medical men disagreed with his methods and findings."

"We've heard of him," Richard said. "And this Doctor Beckwith? He wishes to do what with Charlotte?"

Maryanne noticed George's hand clasping Emily's during the conversation. How anxious she must be for her sister. Maryanne gave her attention to Mr Mathieson again.

"I'm sorry but I don't know…" he glanced at Emily before continuing. "But I do not trust him. He seems to have become more obsessive."

Maryanne had to ask a question bothering her.

"Mr Mathieson – what part has Mr Taylor played in this?"

"I'm still as puzzled as you are. He professed a fondness for Miss Harrington, although she does not return it, and he introduced me to Doctor Beckwith. But he now appears to be assisting the doctor to abduct Charlotte."

"And as we know, not everything is always as we suppose," Maryanne said.

She had never trusted Mr Taylor but wondered if he was so weak that he had allowed the doctor influence over him. Or perhaps he had an ulterior reason.

"Well, he most certainly shall not set foot in this house again," Lady Malden said.

"But what can we do to find Charlotte?" Emily asked again. "This talking is not rescuing my sister!"

"You are correct, Emily." Richard stood. "I'd be grateful if you will direct me to where they may have taken the girl, Mathieson, for we cannot leave here there."

Mr Mathieson nodded and stood up. "We can go forthwith."

"Will you go now, this evening?" Emily asked.

"I think we must, or we will not rest," Richard assured her.

Maryanne smiled at her beloved and wished she might go with them. Although... that might be possible.

"Why don't we take the carriage," she suggested.

"We?" Richard glanced at her, eyebrows raised.

Maryanne stood straight as she replied. "Charlotte

will need a female's company and I wish to go with you."

Before he could reply or argue, Emily cried out. "Oh, could you do that, Maryanne? You are so much more practical than I, and Charlotte will be glad of your presence."

"You see?" Maryanne said to Richard and everyone else. "It is settled. Shall we make ready?"

"If you are quite certain, Maryanne, please wrap up warmly," Lady Malden said. "My carriage is at your disposal."

Richard waited until Lady Malden went to ring for the footman before confronting Maryanne in a lowered voice.

"This is foolhardy, Maryanne. We don't know what we might face."

"Which is why I must go with you, for I should worry myself ill. Besides, Charlotte *will* need a woman's touch."

Richard gently touched her face. "I confess I cannot argue with your reasoning. But promise you'll remain vigilant and keep beside me."

"I promise to do my best to obey your request."

Her wording had not escaped him as he took her hand.

"I could not bear it if anything happened to you, Maryanne."

"I know, for that is how I feel. We are better together. But let's not waste any more time. We must find poor Charlotte."

George coughed and added his suggestion. "I'd be happy to go with you, Richard, if it would help."

Richard glanced at Emily before replying. "Thank

you, but I think you will be required here, brother."

Emily took George's arm. "Please stay and keep me company while we wait, if you will."

Since George could not deny Emily anything, it was settled.

Maryanne took her farewell from a tearful Emily, thankful her cousin had George by her side.

"Please bring my sister safely home," Emily whispered.

Maryanne nodded. She had no idea if they would even find Charlotte right away, but must remain hopeful. Richard and Mr Mathieson were discussing the quickest way to their destination, assuming Mr Mathieson knew exactly where Charlotte would be held.

It might be a difficult, or even dangerous night ahead but Maryanne was determined to play her part in ensuring the safe return of her cousin.

Chapter Seventeen

The road was dark and bumpy as the carriage rolled through the night with only a lantern at either side lighting their way. Maryanne rested her head against Richard's broad shoulder, wishing it were in other circumstances.

"We shall go straight to the doctor's establishment," Mr Mathieson had suggested. "I cannot imagine where else Charlotte might be."

"Alone with those two men?" Maryanne asked, horrified at the idea.

"I believe there is a housekeeper and an older female cousin who lives with him."

That was something at least, if Charlotte were chaperoned. But she did not want to dwell on what might be happening to the poor girl.

"His house is a little way from the city but near enough for his work with patients, and to bring them home for further observation when necessary," Mr Mathieson explained.

"You seem to know a great deal about the doctor and his methods," Maryanne could not resist observing.

"I recently discovered he treated my sister at one time." Mr Mathieson looked away and said no more.

Maryanne stayed silent, aware it was too painful a subject but she had more sympathy for him now, having seen the doctor.

Fortunately, Lady Malden's coachman was an experienced driver and native of London and its surrounds and had assured them he would find the way from the directions. Maryanne tried not to yawn too frequently after the tiring evening. Perhaps if she rested her eyes for a few moments...

"Maryanne, we are here," Richard gently woke her and smiled when she startled.

"Oh, I had not meant to fall asleep!"

"It's as well you've rested even for a short time as it's going to be a long night."

Maryanne sat up, tidied her hair and nodded across to Mr Mathieson who was fastening his coat. Quite how they were to proceed once alighted from the carriage, she had not an idea. Fortunately, that was not up to her.

The house stood in its own grounds through large open gates and the carriage stopped out of sight of the front door. Maryanne shivered, not only from the cold night air. Would they indeed find her cousin in such a place? She was grateful the coachman was a strong-looking burly man and doubtless in possession of a weapon of some kind for protection, although she fervently hoped he would have no need to use such an item.

She stared at the dark façade of the imposing house. Most of the windows were in darkness but at least two were candlelit from within. From what Mr Mathieson had told them, it served as both a home and a treatment establishment, which did nothing to reassure her.

Although she had read some of the more lurid Gothic novels, Maryanne tried not to let her imagination run too far ahead of her. Even at Mulberry

Manor, where Charlotte's problems had begun, she had not believed the evidence of her own eyes at first.

However, the present was enough concern for now and she asked the two gentlemen how they should proceed.

"I imagine the household will be abed by now, "Richard said.

"There is one ploy we might try," Mr Mathieson peered at Maryanne. "If Miss Robertson were to knock first and ask for admittance, I cannot suppose anyone would refuse at this time of night."

"No, I will not let Maryanne put herself in danger," Richard said at once.

Maryanne touched Richard's arm but turned to the other man. "I agree with your suggestion, Mr Mathieson. I assume you both mean to join me at some point?"

"Exactly. We shall be half-hidden to the side in the darkness."

Richard shook his head but said no more and Maryanne knew it was their best chance of admittance. She hoped a footman or housekeeper would answer the door, lest the doctor recognised her.

Ensuring they were out of sight of the doorway, the two men waited while Maryanne approached the large wooden doors. She had pulled the hood of her cloak over her hair and trusted she would not be mistaken for a vagrant.

Heart beating too fast, but fully committed to rescuing Charlotte, she rapped the door knocker. Silence, apart from her nervous breathing. She tried again. If they were abed, it would take time to reach the door.

As she glanced across at Richard, the door creaked open and Maryanne was confronted by a sleepy-looking elderly footman.

"Yes? What d'you want?"

Resolving to be as commanding as possible, Maryanne drew her hood back.

"I must speak to the doctor immediately."

The man peered at her suspiciously. "Why d'you want to see him at this time of night?"

"It is a matter of great delicacy and I must insist."

Her tone must have been enough to convince him, for he stepped aside after opening the door further. Although she grimaced in distaste at the way his droopy eyes looked over her abdomen as though suspecting the type of delicate situation to which she alluded.

Before he could begin closing the door, Maryanne put her hand against her forehead and sagged against the wall. "Please help me."

While the man stared helplessly at Maryanne, Richard and Mr Mathieson stepped into the hall.

"Hoi! What's the meaning of this?" the footman cried, at the same time slinking backwards from them.

"We mean you no harm, sir, but we must speak with the doctor at once." Richard turned to Maryanne. "Are you well enough?"

Understanding that she was still to pretend to need the doctor's assistance, she touched a hand to her forehead again. "If only I could see Doctor Beckwith."

Surmising he had no option, the footman shuffled along the hall, candle held high. "You'd better come with me then. Though the master won't be pleased at the interruption."

Richard put his arm around Maryanne as they followed. She leant against him as though for support, to keep up the pretence.

Would they soon find Charlotte? Maryanne had tried not to believe that her cousin might be in London already and not here at all. But it seemed the doctor was at home which gave her hope.

However, the footman merely showed them into a dull drawing room, the fire already out, and Maryanne shivered again.

"How do we find Charlotte?" she asked, once the footman had departed.

"We shall see what the doctor has to say first. Perhaps he'll realise his folly in taking her away," Richard suggested.

"If there is any denial, I promise I'm not leaving this house without Charlotte, even if we have to search from top to bottom," Mr Mathieson said.

Maryanne was surprised at his passion and understood his affection for her cousin was no doubt genuine.

"Let us hope it doesn't come to that," Maryanne said. She did not want to remain in this house longer than necessary.

At that very moment, the door was thrust open and a very angry doctor strode into the room, leaving the door ajar.

Chapter Eighteen

"What is the meaning of this? How dare you arrive at my home, uninvited, at this time of night!"
Richard faced the doctor, his height diminishing the other.

"We have come to take Miss Harrington home." His voice did not waver as he stared at the doctor.

"Don't know what you mean," the doctor blustered. "This is my home and I was informed that a young woman required my help." He glared at Maryanne.

"I do need your help, Doctor Beckwith," Maryanne said in a clear voice. "My cousin was abducted by you this evening and we are here to take her home."

"What nonsense is this? How dare you make such an accusation." The doctor turned his back on Richard as he sneered at Maryanne.

But Mr Mathieson approached the doctor until he stood face to face.

"I witnessed the abduction. You and your accomplice, Mr Taylor, took this young lady's cousin away in your carriage earlier this evening. And we have already alerted the police."

Maryanne's estimation of Mr Mathieson rose even more when he sounded completely convincing; threatening in a quiet but determined manner.

But the doctor was not giving in so easily. "You're gravely mistaken. This is my home, as I've stated before, and I must ask you to leave."

Maryanne tried to think how they might go upstairs. Perhaps once in the hall, she could contrive to search.

"Perhaps you *were* mistaken, Mr Mathieson, and we should go," Maryanne said.

No wonder Richard was looking puzzled at her capitulating so quickly, but she hoped he would follow her lead.

Before they could leave, however, the doctor peered at Mr Mathieson.

"Mathieson? D'you not have a sister who was very interested in my work? She even began to learn how to mesmerise others and was a good patient *and* student, until she ceased to visit."

The silence at his words was palpable as all three stared at the doctor.

Mr Mathieson glared. "You did know my sister then?" His eyes narrowed. "It was *you* who influenced her mind so that she quite lost her reason. But you do not know she is dead?"

The doctor suddenly took a step back as though sensing the change in atmosphere.

"You shall not ruin another young woman's life. Stand aside!"

Mr Mathieson would not be stopped. He had no need to push the doctor from his path as he strode towards the door, Richard and Maryanne in his wake. For the doctor had already whirled round and rushed ahead.

"Search upstairs," Mr Mathieson said, as he took the stairs two at a time. "Check every room, no matter to whom it belongs."

Maryanne was happy to oblige, more than ever convinced that Charlotte was within.

As they reached one of many upstairs rooms, a door opened and a woman peered out, candle in hand.

"What is this noise? Who's there?" she called.

Maryanne stopped abruptly, Richard behind her. She recognised the face beneath the night cap, although she looked older and plainer.

"Madame Juliette?"

Although she barely resembled the exotic woman she had seen before, Maryanne knew this was the spiritualist from their first night at Lady Malden's house, and from the soirée when she had been accompanied both times by none other than Mr Taylor.

Chapter Nineteen

"I asked what's all this noise? Why are *you* here?" The woman neither agreed with nor denied Maryanne's recognition.

"Where is Mr Taylor?" Maryanne asked, ignoring her question.

"How should I know?"

Mr Mathieson could no longer remain silent. "We are looking for a young lady whom the doctor abducted and we believe her to be here."

The sharp gaze wavered. "What? In my room? Preposterous!"

Maryanne noticed there was no denial about the presence of a young lady.

"Madame Juliette," she began. "This is a very serious matter. My cousin is in a delicate state of mind. Even now, Lady Malden will be informing the police of the abduction by Doctor Beckwith and Mr Taylor."

"My nephew has nothing to do with this," Madame Juliette said, drawing her shawl around her.

"Nephew?" At first Maryanne supposed she referred to the doctor, but then realised it must be Mr Taylor.

"He has certainly played some part in the abduction but we only wish to take my cousin home."

While Maryanne had been talking, she was aware that Mr Mathieson had edged further along in the dim corridor. Next minute, he called out.

"I've found her! Quick, come and help me, Carmichael."

Maryanne hurried after Richard as he ran towards another, less obvious door, at the end of the corridor. Her heart chilled when she heard a woman scream. Charlotte!

Within the room, Mr Mathieson was struggling with Mr Taylor while the doctor was about to administer a binding to Charlotte's mouth. Her wild-eyed stare focused on Maryanne with a silent cry for help.

"Take your hands away from my cousin, Doctor," she said. "It is over."

A quick glance at Richard and Mr Mathieson confirmed they had overcome Mr Taylor and secured his hands with another binding.

As Maryanne hurried to Charlotte, Madame Juliette stood at the door, the candle illuminating her pale face.

"William? What have you to do with this young lady?"

Mr Taylor grinned at his aunt. "Don't try to act innocent, Aunt *Jane*, you old harridan. You were the one who told cousin John about the girl. But it's gone too far this time. This one has too many connections to disappear or end up in the asylum."

Madame Juliette's smile chilled Maryanne even more. "I knew you were growing too fond of this girl, nephew. Did you think you had a chance with someone like her, you poor deluded fool? It's only my money that keeps you in fancy clothes and allows you to mix in society."

Mr Taylor's arrogant grin disappeared. "And I've

been earning every penny by gleaning enough information for your séances, as well as subjects for the doctor, until I could earn enough money to leave you all behind. Without me, you'll soon be discovered for the fraud you are."

During this diatribe, Maryanne had been helping Charlotte to her feet while listening to the aunt and nephew argue. But no one had been looking at the doctor and Maryanne now discovered he had sidled silently from the room at some point.

"Where has the doctor gone?" she asked.

Madame Juliette smiled at them all. "He's too wily for you, is cousin John. Now take the girl and go while you still can. But let my nephew be."

Maryanne helped Charlotte to the door, her only desire to take her back to Lady Malden's.

"Come," Richard said. "There is nothing to be gained from remaining here." He turned to Mr Taylor and his aunt. "But rest assured your names will be known and a warning circulated about the doctor. Lady Malden has great influence in society."

Maryanne wondered whether the threat would make much difference. No doubt Madame Juliette was in demand as a medium at the popular spiritualist evenings, while the doctor must be well-known to have spoken at the Crystal Palace. Although he had now overstepped himself with abducting her cousin against her will.

As for Mr Taylor, she suspected he would disappear from society for a short time.

Charlotte appeared to be in shock but it was to Mr Mathieson she turned once they had reached the doors. She allowed him to support her all the way to the carriage. Maryanne had to be content that her cousin was so at ease with him after her experience. She hoped Charlotte might be able to tell them what had happened but knew not to press her too soon.

They all remained silent at first in the carriage home, Charlotte still half-leaning against Mr Mathieson's shoulder, her eyes closed.

Then Mr Mathieson spoke softly to Maryanne and Richard. "Forgive me for thinking Mr Taylor only wished to help Charlotte. We met at a meeting about mesmerism, although the doctor was not present, and Taylor told me he knew the leading specialist on the subject. Little did I know then how well my sister had known Doctor Beckwith."

Maryanne had to curtail her impatience to know more about what had happened to Charlotte and was glad of Richard's shoulder close to her own. No doubt Emily would have questions enough and it was best to allow Charlotte this peace, outwardly at least. She could not imagine what the girl must be feeling by now and could only pray there was no irreversible damage to her cousin's already fragile mind.

Yet, as she caught Mr Mathieson's eye and observed his tenderness with Charlotte, she hoped the girl might find a measure of happiness in the future.

Their return journey seemed quicker and soon the carriage was drawing up at Lady Malden's house. They had scarcely reached the door when George opened it.

"Oh, thank the Lord you are safe home, Charlotte," he cried, ushering them inside. "Lady Malden sent the footman to bed since he rises early, and I could not rest. You must all be exhausted."

Before they even reached the drawing room, Emily came rushing to her sister.

"Oh, Charlotte, you are safe!" And she hugged her tight.

Maryanne noticed that Charlotte barely reacted, but just then Lady Malden joined them and addressed them in her no-nonsense manner.

"You have done well to bring Charlotte back to us. Now, this young lady needs to go straight to bed. All questions can wait until tomorrow."

Maryanne silently applauded the lady's good sense. Charlotte was in no fit state to speak to anyone as far as she could see.

"Come, Emily and I shall see you settled, Charlotte," Maryanne said. She turned to Richard and Mr Mathieson. "Thank you both for rescuing my cousin."

Richard nodded. "You played a very big part in our success, Maryanne."

He and George took their leave, promising to call upon them the next day.

Just as Maryanne wondered if Mr Mathieson was lodging nearby, the gentleman also took his leave. It was the only time Charlotte reacted when Mr Mathieson took her hand.

"I'm glad you're safe, my dear. Rest now and I shall call upon you tomorrow, with Lady Malden's consent."

"You are welcome here at any time, Mr Mathieson. Now I shall bid you all goodnight before morning arrives."

Charlotte watched Mr Mathieson leave before allowing Maryanne and Emily to lead her upstairs.

Once in her room, she prepared for bed as though in a trance, neither speaking nor looking directly at them.

Maryanne began to fear the girl was perhaps still under the doctor's influence until Charlotte suddenly cried out.

"Don't leave me alone, Emily. Will you sleep here with me please?"

At once, Emily hurried to her sister's side. "Of course, my dearest sister. I shall remain by your side for as long as you need me."

A loud sob escaped Charlotte as she made space for Emily beside her.

Maryanne smiled at them both, relieved to hear Charlotte speak at last, even in obvious distress. "Goodnight, my dearest cousins."

Not daring to think how much of the night had already passed, Maryanne climbed wearily into bed. Perhaps her sister's love was exactly what Charlotte most needed for now at least. And it would seem that she had formed a strong attachment to Mr Mathieson, odd as it seemed to her.

Yet, his sister and Charlotte had both come under the influence of the doctor and one had been lost forever.

Maryanne's thoughts and memories threatened to keep her awake for what remained of the night. What would become of Charlotte now? Exactly what had the doctor done to her? Unless they had been in time. It might be some days before they made sense of it and by then, they would be back at Mulberry Manor.

Burrowing under the covers, Maryanne allowed her thoughts to turn at last to Richard and their too soon parting. What did the future hold for herself? With these happier musings, Maryanne finally drifted into dreams.

Chapter Twenty

Their leave-taking from Lady Malden was a mixture of sadness and relief at taking Charlotte home to recover.

"You must send word to me, Maryanne, once you are safely at Mulberry Manor. And, Emily, please tell your mother and father to let me know how Charlotte progresses."

Maryanne was as warmly embraced as her cousins and was pleased to have met the wise and kind Lady Malden.

It was her farewell from Richard that saddened Maryanne the most, until he promised to visit her and her parents within the month.

"I don't want to waste any more time apart than necessary," he said, kissing her on both cheeks while in view of the others.

George similarly said farewell to Emily who had not left her sister's side. But the biggest surprise was when Mr Mathieson arrived in time to see Charlotte, promising to keep in touch with her and hoping to see her again one day soon.

Then they were on their way to the railway station. As Maryanne watched the passing London streets, her thoughts were divided between concern for Charlotte and excitement at Richard's proposed visit to her home. But first she was happy to make a stop at Mulberry Manor for two nights with her cousins before continuing her journey to the Scottish Borders.

Her aunt and uncle were overjoyed to welcome them back, wrapping each of the girls in a tight embrace. Yet, Maryanne observed that Mrs Harrington was aware something ailed her elder daughter.

Although she answered when spoken to, Charlotte still had a far-away look in her eyes and a lack of concentration. When she had retired early to bed, Emily accompanying her, Maryanne explained as well as she could.

"And this doctor tried to experiment on my child?" Mrs Harrington was outraged while her husband shook his head.

"But you found her in time, Maryanne?"

"I believe so, but that was all due to Mr Mathieson."

Her aunt and uncle could scarcely believe the gentleman had entered their daughter's life again and it was only when Maryanne spoke warmly of his tenderness towards Charlotte that they were willing to listen without anger.

"And he wishes to visit our daughter here? What do you make of that, Maryanne?" her uncle asked at last.

Flattered to be asked her opinion but aware it was too much responsibility, she thought carefully before replying.

"I think perhaps Charlotte would be happier to see him. He may be the very person to find out exactly what happened."

Mr Harrington spoke before his wife for a change. "Then we shall invite him to come and stay for a few days, if you will consent to remain here until then, my dear."

Although anxious to return home to await Richard's visit, Maryanne was curious to know more about Charlotte's experience. Mr Mathieson might be glad of her presence since she knew how sincerely he cared for her cousin.

"Of course, I shall, uncle. I expect Mama and Papa will scarcely have noticed my absence." Besides, she needed to reassure herself that Charlotte would recover well enough.

The days were already becoming shorter now that September had arrived, but the gardens still retained enough interest, even as some of the trees began to shed their leaves. Maryanne passed the time in pleasant strolls with Emily when the late autumn sunshine deigned to visit for a time. Evenings gave her time to write in her journal and to enjoy a few solitary walks around the grounds of the old manor house to gaze at the stars before bedtime, wishing Richard was with her.

And all the while, Charlotte seldom left her room, except to eat with them. Emily spent much of her time with her sister who only responded to general conversation if addressed directly. Even Emily could learn no more about Charlotte's experience in London but she still slept in her sister's room.

Then word came that Mr Mathieson would arrive the following day and Charlotte suddenly brightened, confirming her strong attachment to the man. Maryanne could only hope he would not let her down, or she feared Charlotte might not survive.

True to his word, Mr Mathieson arrived by carriage the next day and was welcomed by Mr and Mrs Harrington in their usual friendly manner. Maryanne admired their spirit, considering this man and his sister had brought so much worry and despair on the previous visit.

"Thank you for allowing me to come here again," Mr Mathieson said. "I only hope I may be of assistance. I care very much for your daughter and want to see her restored."

"A very pretty speech, sir," Mrs Harrington said, but without rancour.

It was soon evident to all, however, that Mr Mathieson was exactly the person Charlotte most needed. From the day he arrived, he and Charlotte spent as much time together as possible, accompanied by either Emily or Maryanne.

It was on one of their strolls along past the gardens, Maryanne keeping a discreet distance, that an incident occurred to make her heart beat faster.

They had walked further than usual beyond the grounds towards the stream and were nearing the bridge when Charlotte appeared to falter. Next minute, she was being held by Mr Mathieson while Maryanne hurried to reach them.

"What is it?" she cried, relieved to see Charlotte still standing, albeit leaning against Mr Mathieson.

"It… it was here, was it not?"

"What was, my dear?" Mr Mathieson asked.

But Maryanne suddenly realised where they were and feared she understood too well what Charlotte asked.

"It was here… where you found me, was it not?" Charlotte covered her eyes before lowering them again to stare around, gaze wild.

"I remember…freezing cold water…drowning."

She stared unseeing at them. "Other memories too." She shivered. "A small space…suffocating…

"Hush, my dear. You are safe," Mr Mathieson said, seemingly to no avail as Charlotte continued to stare as though reliving past horrors.

Maryanne did not want to intrude and watched as Mr Mathieson stood directly in front of Charlotte taking her hands in his.

"Look at me, Charlotte. You are not alone and no one can hurt you. You are perfectly safe."

Maryanne could have no doubt that Mr Mathieson knew exactly how to speak to her cousin and only prayed it was always with the best of intentions.

Gradually, Charlotte looked at Mr Mathieson with understanding in her eyes and she took a deep sobbing breath.

"I will never let anyone hurt or frighten you again," Mr Mathieson promised.

"I am safe," she said. "But your poor sister…"

Maryanne heard the tender note in Charlotte's voice and knew she was at last being restored to them.

"It was for the best, my dear," Mr Mathieson said, taking Charlotte in his arms for a moment.

Accepting his arm, Charlotte agreed to return to the manor. Maryanne noticed she glanced once more at the spot where she had almost lost her life on Mr Mathieson's previous visit. And she wondered if the spectre of his poor deluded sister had haunted them both for too long.

Chapter Twenty-one

Over the final days of Maryanne's visit, Charlotte improved a little more, especially when Mr Mathieson was with her. Whatever memories and fragments of horror had disturbed her for the past year or so seemed to be fading, or most of them at least.

At last, she was able to try and tell them what had happened after her abduction.

"Doctor Beckwith had discovered I was easily mesmerised and he wanted to use me in his further experiments so he could prove its worth as a treatment."

Charlotte stopped, unable to go on for a moment until Mr Mathieson took her hand.

"Rather than helping me only to confront my nightmares, as Mr Taylor had promised, the doctor soon wished to inflict pain on my body, ensuring me I would not feel anything."

Maryanne's horrified gaze met Emily's, as she remembered the pin pushed into Charlotte's hand at the Crystal Palace. Did he then mean to escalate that experiment?

"But he did not actually succeed in hurting you, did he?" she asked.

Charlotte shook her head. "Only because you, dear cousin, came to rescue me with two heroes at your side."

Although thankful that Charlotte was now able to

speak of her experience, Maryanne suspected there was still much healing to be accomplished.

One morning, Charlotte surveyed her sister, Maryanne and Mr Mathieson over breakfast before making a request.

"Will you come with me to that room, please? I need to face the past before I can truly move on with my future."

Maryanne agreed with the sense of it, for it was only in facing fears that that they might overcome them, or so she hoped. And she had noticed the meaningful glance between Charlotte and Mr Mathieson when she mentioned the future.

"We shall all accompany you, Charlotte," Maryanne said.

"It will be good for me too," Mr Mathieson said.

When they were going upstairs, Emily held back with Maryanne so she could confide in her.

"Charlotte has never entered that room since, and I don't wonder at her for I do not like to go there myself."

The guest bedroom had been kept clean and tidy but Maryanne noticed the other smaller door was now exposed and wondered if her cousin might hesitate.

Charlotte took a deep breath and, hand on Mr Mathieson's arm, she stepped inside to glance around.

"It is only a room," she said at last. "An empty room." To their astonishment, she marched straight to the other door and, after the smallest hesitation, threw it open. "As is this."

Charlotte's whole demeanour was lighter when they returned downstairs, as though a heavy burden had been removed.

Maryanne could not condone what Mr Taylor had done in introducing Charlotte to the doctor for his experimentation, but perhaps it was the catalyst that had begun Charlotte's recovery. She glanced at Mr Mathieson. Or perhaps her cousin had found love at last, and the gentleman's regret, or guilt, about his sister had been lifted. Doubtless they would find a way to move on together.

Maryanne was making preparations to leave Mulberry Manor at last when they received a happy surprise. She had heard a carriage arrive but could not see enough from her window. Hearing voices, she descended the stairs and there, being relieved of his coat and hat, was Richard Carmichael.

"Good day, Maryanne," he said, on catching sight of her. "I thought we might travel back to Scotland together."

Maryanne's heart soared, both at seeing him and thought of him returning north with her.

"I should like that very much." She tried to control the extent of her pleasure but their eyes conveyed so much more as she took his outstretched hands.

"Well, that sounds like an excellent plan, my dears," Mrs Harrington said, almost clapping her hands in delight.

Richard was kind enough to spare a thought for Emily, who looked crestfallen that George had not accompanied him.

"My brother sends his regards, Emily, and apologises that he had to remain in London a little longer. However, he is soon to join me at Carmichael Hall and I expect he'll break his journey here first."

Emily's lips curved in her sweet smile and

Maryanne knew her cousin would be counting the days until George's arrival.

At last, Maryanne and Richard were ready to set off to Scotland for their respective homes. With much leave taking and promises that Maryanne would send word of her safe arrival, and take her aunt and uncle's warm affections to her dear Mama and Papa, they eventually sat back in the carriage.

Maryanne could not remove her gaze from Richard's as they sat across from each other, enclosed in their own private world.

"Will you remain long at Carmichael Hall?" Maryanne asked, trying to calm her fast-beating heart.

"That depends on several important details," Richard teased.

"Oh. You are not certain of being there for long?"

Instead of replying, Richard moved across to sit beside her when the carriage was on a less bumpy part of the road.

"The most important consideration involves you, Maryanne." He took both her hands, smiling in a way that caught her breath.

"In what way?" she whispered.

"If you will marry me before the year is over, Maryanne Robertson, and live with me at Carmichael Hall, for I cannot bear to be parted from you much longer."

Maryanne gasped but before she could reply, Richard arms were around her as his lips claimed hers.

The tingling inside her increased Maryanne's passion and she returned his kisses until they were tightly bound together.

Finally drawing breath, they stared at each other.

"I assume you're agreeing?" Richard kept his arm around her.

"I am. I want nothing more than to marry you and never be parted again, Richard Carmichael."

Drawing her against his shoulder, he tenderly smoothed her hair from her forehead before kissing her brow. "Then I shall speak to your father when we reach the parsonage, and perhaps your mother will not be too distressed at a wedding within so few months."

"I think both Mama and Papa will be glad we shall not be too far away from them."

"Then, my darling, we have much to plan and discuss, and I suppose we must tell your cousins and my brother," Richard mused.

Maryanne could scarcely think at all except for imagining being married to this wonderful man sooner than she had hoped.

"And I had better organise a wedding gown."

"Meanwhile, I think I should sit across from you again, lest we precipitate the wedding night. But first…"

Reluctantly, Maryanne let him go, aware her own passion had been ignited after another even deeper kiss. But she had waited this long and the joy would be even more abundant when they could remain in each other's arms for as long as they wished.

She gave a fleeting thought to last Christmas at Carmichael Hall when a dangerous charade had played out, yet also brought happiness to others. And to the previous Twelfth Night when she and Richard had fallen in love at Mulberry Manor, in the midst of ghostly fears and tragedy.

She smiled as she met Richard's loving gaze. This

year at Christmas, if all proceeded as they planned, she would take her place by his side as mistress of Carmichael Hall. And she would not allow anything to spoil their happiness.

Acknowledgements and Author's Note

My grateful thanks to V Gemmell for her excellent suggestions, kind corrections, and proof reading to make this novella a better read. Continued thanks to my friends, writing and otherwise, who support, encourage and inspire in equal measure.

As always, my love and thanks to dear husband, Simon, who has always been there for me, supporting me in so many ways.

I first mentioned mesmerism in *Mischief at Mulberry Manor* and it was such a fascinating part of Victorian life, along with spiritualism, that I wanted to explore more as well as rounding off Charlotte's story.

Mesmerism was named after German physician Franz Anton Mesmer who believed in the transference of a natural energy between animate and inanimate objects, first referred to as 'animal magnetism'. He was popular from the late eighteenth to early nineteenth century.

Doctor Elliotson, who is mentioned in the novella, was a professor at University College London and senior physician to University College Hospital in the 1830s, and was the first doctor in Britain to use the stethoscope. If anyone wants to read further on the subject, I can recommend *The Mesmerist* by Wendy Moore.

Dark Delusion is the third Maryanne Mystery novella set in the mid-Victorian era and features some of the characters who were previously involved in Mischief at Mulberry Manor and Christmas Charade.

About the Author

Rosemary Gemmell lives in central Scotland and is the author of historical and contemporary novels, novellas and tween books. She is also a prize-winning freelance writer of short stories, articles and poetry, many published in UK magazines, the USA, and online.

Rosemary is a member of the Society of Authors, the Romantic Novelists' Association and the Scottish Association of Writers. She has a Masters in Literature and History, and Diploma in European Humanities.

You can subscribe to a newsletter on her website for up-to-date news and occasional special offers and giveaways.

You can also connect with her on Facebook and Twitter.

Published Books

Highcrag
The Highland Lass
Return to Kilcraig
Dangerous Deceit
Midwinter Masquerade
Mischief at Mulberry Manor
Christmas Charade
Pride & Progress
Venetian Interlude
The Aphrodite and Adonis Touch

Short Story Collections
Beneath the Treetops
End of the Road
Two of a Kind

Non-Fiction Articles
Scottish People and Places

Middle Grade Children's Fiction
Summer of the Eagles
The Jigsaw Puzzle
The Pharaoh's Gold

Printed in Great Britain
by Amazon

75703667R00090